"I'll neve~~r~~ ~~...~~ **had to die."**

"And how long do you think you'll live once you stick your nose out there asking questions?"

Oh, he was mad. Well, so was she.

"I've waited way too long for someone else to fix this!" she yelled. "You and your BFF Donahue aren't any use, since you're fixated on me. I can't trust anybody in the department. And what were you doing here today, anyway? Hoping I'd lead you to my coconspirators? And then, heck, they tried to abduct me instead. What a disappointment."

Jaw hard, he said, "Are you done?"

"For the moment."

"I followed because I was afraid for you." She felt shame creep over her. She knew why he'd been here today, and it had nothing to do with suspecting her.

"I know," she mumbled. He had betrayed her trust in one way, but she'd always known he wouldn't hurt her, or allow anyone else to hurt her.

TRUSTING THE SHERIFF

USA TODAY Bestselling Author

JANICE KAY JOHNSON

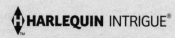

My thanks to Victoria Curran for persuading me to try to write
an Amish story! Here I am on my third, still having fun.

ISBN-13: 978-1-335-60423-1

Trusting the Sheriff

Recycling programs
for this product may
not exist in your area.

Printed in U.S.A.

™ www.Harlequin.com

An author of more than ninety books for children and adults (more than seventy-five for Harlequin), **Janice Kay Johnson** writes about love and family, and pens books of gripping romantic suspense. A *USA TODAY* bestselling author and an eight-time finalist for the Romance Writers of America RITA® Award, she won a RITA® Award in 2008. A former librarian, Janice raised two daughters in a small town north of Seattle, Washington.

Books by Janice Kay Johnson

Harlequin Intrigue

Hide the Child
Trusting the Sheriff

Harlequin Superromance

A Hometown Boy
Anything for Her
Where It May Lead
From This Day On
One Frosty Night
More Than Neighbors
Because of a Girl
A Mother's Claim
Plain Refuge
Her Amish Protectors
The Hero's Redemption
Back Against the Wall

Brothers, Strangers

The Closer He Gets
The Baby He Wanted

The Mysteries of Angel Butte

Bringing Maddie Home
Everywhere She Goes
All a Man Is
Cop by Her Side
This Good Man

Visit the Author Profile page at Harlequin.com.

CAST OF CHARACTERS

Detective Abby Baker—She takes refuge with her Amish family after an ambush leaves her partner dead and her wounded and with a hole in her memory. Bad enough her sergeant distrusts her, but now a killer has followed her to Amish country.

Sheriff Caleb Tanner—He lets an old friend talk him into investigating Abby Baker's secrets. How can he be falling for her, when she may have betrayed and murdered her own partner?

Detective Neal Walker—He died in the alley the night Abby was wounded. Somebody is sure he'd shared his worries and suspicion with his new partner.

Sergeant Michael Donahue—He blames Abby for whatever happened in that alley. Having lost one detective, he's determined to put all the pressure he can on the newest detective in his unit, the one so conveniently claiming amnesia.

Detective Sam Kirk—He offers sympathy and friendship to Abby, but is he playing the role of the good cop to the sergeant's bad cop? Or is he interested in her for another reason altogether?

Nancy and Eli Kemp—They gladly offer a home to their niece even when their Amish ways are violated by the violence that follows her.

Prologue

Footsteps. Night made murky by filtered light. A stench. Agony in her head.

"Why? Why would you do this?" Angry male voice. She knew it, but her mind wouldn't quite supply a face or name. "Tell me before—"

Gunfire blasted. Once, twice.

She managed to fumble a hand toward her unsnapped holster. Empty. Why was it empty? She could see booted feet move, the back of someone crouching over—she couldn't remember who lay still now.

Darkness beckoned and she moaned. When the footsteps approached, it took everything she had to open her eyes a slit. The toes of the boots were inches away. He must be looking down at her.

From somewhere, a voice yelled, "Hey! I called 9-1-1."

Crack. The impact of the bullet bounced her body on the pavement. Pain blossomed like hot red lava.

I'm dead.

Crack.

Chapter One

A hammer pounded Abigail Baker's head. Again. Again. Wasn't the nail in yet?

Pain washed her body, but with her eyes still closed, she homed in on the hot points. Shoulder. Middle of her chest beneath her breasts. Spike through her head.

Someone had applied super glue to her eyelids, but she succeeded in prying them open. She stared blankly upward at an unfamiliar ceiling, then rolled her eyes to see to each side. Her head let her know that she really shouldn't move it.

Curtains surrounded the bed. Abby could just see an IV pole out of the corner of her eye. White, waffle-weave blankets covered her.

Hospital.

The curtain rings rattled and a sturdily built middle-aged woman appeared at the side of her bed. Beaming, she said, "You're awake! Oh, my. How do you feel, dear?"

Abby worked her bone-dry mouth and finally moaned, "Hurt."

"You're with us. Excellent. I need you to wait just a few minutes for the pain relief. The doctor will want to talk to you first."

A hint of temper increased the force of the hammer blows. Note to self: *Don't get mad*. She sank into a near doze, feeling every beat of her heart, conscious of her shallow breaths, floating on the sea of pain.

"Abigail?" A man's voice.

It was a fraction easier to open her eyes this time.

"I'm told you hurt."

"Yes."

"Can you tell me where? Or show me?"

She tried to move her mouth.

"Let me give you some ice chips."

He gently tipped some into her mouth. The cool moisture was nirvana. While she sucked on them, she lifted her right hand, seeing that the IV was in it. She studied it for a minute, then touched her head, her shoulder—feeling a thick dressing—and her breastbone—no padding. Why not, when it hurt, too?

"Good," he said with obvious satisfaction.

She had to work to focus on his face. He was lean, blond with grey hair at his temples. Lived-in face.

"Why am I here?"

Hazel eyes narrowed a flicker. "Do you remember what happened?"

Impatient, Abby made the mistake of starting to shake her head. Pain exploded, and she groaned.

He was suddenly closer. "There's a button here you can push when you need pain relief." He said some more things, but she didn't listen, because he'd put the button in her hand. She squeezed it, and felt relief flooding from her neck to her fingers and toes. Another squeeze, and her headache receded enough for her to think about what he'd asked—and what she'd asked.

"No."

"What's the last thing you do remember?"

That took some concentration. "Laundry. Basement of my building. Someone dumped my clothes and stole the dryer cycle."

He grinned. "I'd remember that, too."

"Partner—Neal—worried about something." After being promoted almost a year ago from patrol to detective in the Major Crimes division of the Kansas City, Missouri, police department, she'd been paired with Neal Walker. His previous partner had just retired. The two of them hit it off, even socializing. Abby and his new wife had become friends. "Wouldn't say." She recalled telling him she'd help, his crooked grin. His voice, tenser than usual. *Let me make sure I'm not imagining things.* He'd dropped her off by her car. And then…

Abby stared into space. And then… There was nothing. Not a single thing. Panic soared and she struggled to sit up.

She and the doctor wrestled briefly. She was so ridiculously weak, he was able to ease her down.

"You need to stay calm," he said soothingly. "Don't worry. People often lose their memories of a period surrounding traumatic events. Right now, your body has to deal with the physical injuries. You've been in a coma, so it's not surprising that your brain isn't entirely booted up yet. Do you understand?"

"Yes." She didn't even blink as she stared at him, afraid to sink into that black void. "How long…?"

"You've been here for three days. We're really happy to see you regaining consciousness."

"What…happened?"

"Your injuries? You were shot twice. Fortunately, you were wearing a Kevlar vest. It didn't stop the bullet in your shoulder, but the shot to your chest might well have killed you. Instead, you have only severe bruising and a cracked sternum. It also appears that when you fell, you struck your head against the corner of a dumpster. I understand you were found in an alley."

Dread supplanted the panic. "Neal?"

The doctor took a step back, his expression becoming guarded. "Your partner?"

"Yes."

"I think I'll let your Sergeant Donahue tell you about that. He's been haunting the place."

She knew. She *knew*.

She managed to turn her face away.

HER DOCTOR DIDN'T allow any visitors until the following day, after they'd moved her from intensive care to a room she currently had to herself. She could only imagine how frustrated Donahue was to be thwarted. Given the severity of her head injury and the length of time she'd spent in a coma, Dr. Sanderlin insisted she rest, use pain medication as needed and not worry.

Yes, he actually said that again. After patting her hand. "Don't worry."

Abby would have done nothing *but* worry if she hadn't felt so rotten. If she didn't push the little button, her head felt like a rocket right at blastoff, spewing fire. If she did use the stuff, she dozed. Quite honestly, she didn't feel much better the day after regaining consciousness, but when she was capable of thinking clearly, she chased herself in circles. What could possibly have happened? If Neal was alive, why wouldn't the doctor have told her so? Or said, *Gosh, I don't know who Neal is?*

And why couldn't she remember?

An orderly had just removed her breakfast tray when she heard a cleared throat and Sergeant Michael Donahue stepped into view. He supervised her unit of detectives, and they all felt lucky. He could be gruff, but never failed to support them against higher-ups or the public when needed. He was smart and capable of compassion, and his detectives very rarely encountered a difficulty he hadn't already met and overcome in his lengthy career.

He'd turned fifty-four back in February, when they threw him a surprise party. Donahue was still a good-looking man, his gray hair short but not buzz-cut. His wife liked to run her fingers through it, he'd tell them with a hidden smile. He dressed well, his suits appearing custom-made to fit his tall body and bulky shoulders, but within an hour or two at the station, he invariably looked rumpled. Abby had met his wife, Jennifer, who was known to roll her eyes on occasion when she dropped by the station and first set eyes on him.

"Abby," he said, his face creased with what she took for concern. "You scared us."

She managed a weak smile.

He pulled a chair close to the bed and lowered himself into it. "Shot twice."

"So they tell me."

The lines on his forehead deepened. "The doctor claims you have no memory of what happened."

"The doctor's right," she said huskily. "I have this huge blank." Her hand rose to touch her temple.

He studied her in silence for longer than she understood. Then he leaned back in the chair and said, "That's a problem for us. The…scene where you were found is puzzling, to put it mildly. I've been hoping you can tell us what occurred."

She gave her head a very careful shake. "I can't. All I know is that I was found in an alley."

"Neal was with you," Donahue said, "also shot twice. Unlike you, he didn't survive."

Yes, she'd known, but the news threw a punch anyway. Abby felt tears burn in her eyes. "How?"

His face hadn't softened at all. She didn't see the expected sympathy. Instead, he had the kind of stony expression suspects saw.

"It appears that you shot Neal with your service weapon and he shot you with his. You apparently struck your head on the dumpster as you fell. You need to tell me if you've been having issues with him, or if he had a problem with how you handled any investigation."

"How *I* handled...?" She gaped at him. "You think we quarreled?"

"How else can you explain the physical evidence?" he said implacably.

"I can't explain anything! Neal and Laura are—were—my best friends! We never disagreed."

"Then why would you have shot him?"

"Did you test for gunpowder residue on my hand?"

He hesitated. "We did, and didn't find any. But the only fingerprints found on your Glock were yours."

Something was very wrong.

"And Neal's?"

"The same."

"There had to have been someone else there," she said, having trouble believing he'd suspect either of them. "You *know* both of us."

"I've seen cops go bad before. It stinks, but it happens. If Neal did, I need you to tell me."

She looked right into his eyes. "I'll never believe he would."

His graying eyebrows rose, obviating any need for him to say what she knew he was thinking: *Then you have to be the bad apple.*

SEVERAL OF ABBY'S fellow detectives came by to see her. Most of them had apparently gathered here at the hospital after she and Neal were found in that alley, holding vigil for her after they learned he was dead. She was told that Sergeant Donahue had worked the scene himself, along with an experienced detective, Sam Kirk. The CSI team had gathered trace evidence—too much of it. Alleys ranked right up there as the most impossible scenes. Employees from businesses along the block came out regularly to drop garbage into a dumpster or smoke a cigarette, grinding the butt out with a shoe and leaving it where it lay. Homeless people lurked, scrounging in the dumpsters, sleeping behind them, having sex and getting into fights. Cars cut through, passengers or drivers tossing litter out windows. Rats frequented the alley, as did stray cats.

The man who'd heard the gunshots and had the guts to run toward them rather than away would have left his own trace evidence. He claimed to have seen a dark shape standing over her, a man—he thought male—who ran away when he called out.

Sergeant Donahue was clearly not convinced the

sole witness hadn't conjured the sight of a villain to make himself appear more heroic.

Laura Walker never came. Abby called her a week after she'd regained consciousness.

"Laura? This is Abby. I wanted to tell you—" She was talking to dead air. A woman she'd considered a good friend had learned of Sergeant Donahue's suspicions and immediately bought into them. What other explanation was there?

That was the first time in a very long while that Abby let herself cry—but only after the lights had gone out and she was alone. Better than falling asleep. Nightmares grabbed her the minute she dropped off. They were lurid and felt important. She'd wake gasping with shock and fear, but couldn't remember any details.

Visits from her coworkers tailed off. They were busy; she understood that. But she wondered if they had any idea how isolated she felt when she trudged up and down the halls of the hospital, trying to regain enough strength to go home. Nurses and orderlies fussed over her, but that was their job. Why hadn't she made more friends? The kind who would stand by her?

But she knew. She'd never quite fit in, wherever she was. Not as a child, migrating between her grandparents' farm and a "normal" life with her silent, wounded father. Certainly not in college, where the sense of morality she'd absorbed from the deeply religious Amish part of her family separated her from other students. And then she became a cop, joining a small minority who were women.

Maybe she hadn't really tried. Was she more comfortable alone? she asked herself, troubled.

Five days after she'd woken from the coma, Dr. Sanderlin told her she was ready to leave the hospital.

"I'll have a social worker stop by to help you form a plan," he assured her. "If you live alone...?"

"Yes."

"You need to have someone around to help you. I'd rather not extend your hospital stay if we can come up with a solution, but I'm not willing to send you off to pass out or fall or have a traumatic flashback where nobody will see. If you don't have family you can go to, I recommend at least a week in a rehab facility."

Her father... No. They stayed in touch, but conversations were always stiff, awkward. She hadn't even let him know yet that she'd been shot. He'd grown up in foster care, and now had no family but her. Her mother's parents, who'd half raised her, were gone, too, but Aenti Nancy and Onkel Eli would take her in. She knew they would. The Amish were like that. They loved visitors, and they took care of the people they loved. Even people they didn't love. If their church community included an irascible old woman who was difficult to like, they took care of her anyway, with generosity, humor and no grumbling. She'd heard her grandfather—her *grossdaadi*—say, "How would we learn to forgive, if the

Lord didn't give us cranky neighbors?" Then he'd grin. "And teenagers."

Of course, she wasn't one of them, never had been, really, even though she'd attended Amish schools for weeks or even, once, several months at a time. She dressed "plain" when she was with her Amish family, grew so accustomed to having no television, she'd never watched much even as an adult. Her grandparents might have hoped she'd choose to be baptized to join their faith, but weren't surprised when she didn't. Especially after what happened to—

No, the past had nothing to do with the here and now. She needed to focus on her next step. Physical recovery, Abby could already tell, was going to be slow. Plus, even if she bounced out of bed feeling great, going back to the job clearly wasn't an option until she could explain what had happened that night in the alley.

If she ever could. The doctor had explained that her memory of the missing week might return in its entirety, she might recall pieces of it…or it might never come back.

Her aunt and uncle would take her in without question, pamper her even as they set her to doing chores she could handle. The idea of sitting at the long table in that big farm kitchen, peeling potatoes or rolling out pie dough while the women chattered and the younger children helped to the extent they were able sounded heavenly to Abby right now.

Her smile felt rusty, but real. *Heavenly?* That might've been a pun, but it was also truth.

She'd call and leave a message on the machine in the phone shanty out by the road that passed her family's farm, and hope Onkel Eli checked it soon so that her arrival wasn't a complete surprise.

Unfortunately, she didn't think she was up to the meandering pace, clouds of exhaust and swaying ride of a bus. Now all she needed was to find a ride.

"LEFT UP AHEAD." All ten families who lived on this gravel road were Amish. Abby felt sure Aenti Nancy would have told her if someone had had to sell out. She wrote to Abby weekly, long, chatty missives that always made her feel as if she mattered.

Despite the bands of pain tightening around her head, excitement fizzed inside her. Abby leaned forward until the seat belt put uncomfortable pressure on her shoulder and chest. She hadn't been here since Thanksgiving, having volunteered to work over the Christmas holidays so that a detective who had children could take the time off. The farm felt like home, more so than her father's house had since her mother died. Why hadn't she visited in the spring? It had been nine, no, ten months since she'd made it to see her family here.

Sam Kirk, the detective working her case, had offered to drive her. She'd fully expected him to grill her during the two-hour drive, but had decided not to look a gift horse in the mouth. Besides, if he could ask the question that would unlock her memories, she'd be as glad as he would.

Sam was in his late thirties or early forties and tended to be quiet, but when he spoke, people listened. He had a presence, she'd long since decided, even though he was lean and not above average height. Abby had always felt shy around him, and hadn't yet had occasion to work closely with him.

When he'd first picked her up, he drove her to her apartment and helped her pack a duffel bag full of clothes. Without complaint, he also carried a tote bag of books she kept meaning to read out to the car.

Returning, he nodded at her laptop. "You'll want that."

"No electricity where I'm going." Seeing his puzzlement, she had to explain why the Amish refused to be on the grid, linked with people who didn't share their faith.

He looked stunned. "No TV? But…the Chiefs' first regular-season game is next weekend."

She laughed at him, relaxing for the first time.

When he offered to come back to dispose of any foods that would rot while she was away and empty the kitchen trash, Abby handed over her key. If he could figure out her laptop password, he was welcome to browse her emails and files. He'd probably search her apartment, but she didn't care. She had nothing to hide. In fact…she didn't have much at all.

The first fifteen minutes of the drive had passed

in silence. Then he broke it. "The sergeant is doing his job, you know."

She stiffened. "I know."

"I go with my gut more than he does, and my gut tells me whatever happened in that alley was a setup."

Good cop, bad cop was her first thought. She knew she was right, but was still susceptible enough to kindness and a pretense of belief in her to give her a lump in her throat. "Thank you for saying that."

He nodded, and asked about physical therapy and whether her headaches were receding. Abby gave him the upbeat answers, refusing to admit that the vibration of the moving vehicle and the occasional bumps had her thinking about hammers again. Just sitting upright tired her.

But seeing the farm now made her forget her tiredness and every ache and pain. She exclaimed, "Oh, the corn looks almost ripe!"

White-painted board fencing separated the fields from the gravel road that showed the narrow tracks made by the steel wheels of Amish buggies. The corn stalks stood tall, topped with fluffy yellow silks surrounding the ears. Last year, corn crops throughout the Midwest had dried up with the drought. Aenti Nancy mentioned the weather in every one of her letters, although she would never complain if it were too dry or wet. The Amish accepted God's purpose, whether they understood it or not. That didn't mean they wouldn't be rejoicing in what promised to be a bumper crop this year.

"Do they grow anything else?" Sam asked, turning into the narrow lane leading up a gentle slope to the house.

"Yes, of course," she said distractedly. "Raspberries, strawberries, soybeans. They have a good-sized orchard of fruit trees, and two black walnut trees. And a kitchen garden, of course. Plus, my aunt and uncle raise a few steers each year, and keep chickens. Most of their food comes from the farm."

He shot her a look from dark eyes. "I'd never have guessed you came from a background like this. You actually wear that getup? Bonnet and all?"

"Yes, when I'm here. I didn't grow up Amish, you know. I just…" There was no reason to explain. She continued, "They wouldn't say anything if I came for a short visit and wore jeans and T-shirts, but I don't." She explained simply, "It wouldn't be respectful."

By the time the car rolled to a stop in front of the white-painted farmhouse with a wraparound porch, two women had rushed out of the front door and a man strode toward them from the huge barn.

Abby scrabbled for the seat-belt release and the car door handle at the same time, eager to leap out.

Sam's hand on her arm slowed her. "Take it easy, Detective. You don't want to collapse at their feet."

She didn't. She climbed out very carefully and, eyes stinging, fell into her aunt's arms. "Aenti Nancy."

"So glad we were to hear you were coming!" her aunt exclaimed. "Excited, we are."

Abby gently pulled free to greet first her cousin Rose, then her uncle, a tall, stern man who nonetheless hugged her and murmured, "You have stayed away too long."

She hugged him back, managing to knock his summer straw hat off. He laughed when he bent to pick it up. Abby transferred her gaze to Rose, who was pregnant. Very pregnant.

"Oh, my! Aenti Nancy told me, but I didn't know you were so far along."

Brown-haired, gray-eyed and tending to plumpness, Rose wrinkled her nose. "The midwife sent me to the doctor for an ultrasound. I'm having twins." She splayed her hands on her sizeable belly. "I still have three months to go, but the doctor said I won't make it that long."

"Girls or boys?"

"One of each, he thought." She beamed. "I drove myself over today even though Matthew doesn't like me going out now, but to have you home!"

Hearing her genuine delight, Abby felt her tears spilling over at last. She used the backs of her hands to swipe at her wet cheeks, introduced Sam to her family and allowed her aunt to usher them into the house.

"Sit, sit!" she told both Abby and Sam, who appeared bemused and a little uncomfortable. A cup of coffee and raspberry pie topped with fresh cream proved irresistible to him, however, and although he stood strong enough to repeat several times that he couldn't stay for dinner, he did accept containers of food that would probably feed him for several days.

His mouth quirked as he said goodbye to Abby. "Don't put on too much weight while you're here. Wouldn't want you to get slow on your feet."

She laughed and said, "Thank you. For bringing me home. It can't be what you wanted to do on your day off." Assuming, her cynical side reminded her, that this hadn't actually been a working day for him. Good cop, remember?

"I was glad to do it," he said, and left.

Abby sat at the kitchen table, inhaling the smell of good things cooking, very aware of Rose reaching out to clasp her hand, her aunt fussing at the stove and Onkel Eli smiling gently at her from his place at the head of the table.

Home.

Chapter Two

Phone to his ear, Caleb Tanner leaned back in his large desk chair and stacked his booted feet on his desk. He thought it unlikely Mike Donahue had called in the middle of a working day for no reason but to catch up, but so far, all they'd done was chitchat—his mother's description for meaningless talk. Fortunately, he was a patient man. He didn't have anywhere he needed to be.

He and Donahue had known each other as Kansas City PD officers, partnering together in the drug-enforcement unit for a couple of years. Undercover work was hell on marriage or having a family—or even meeting a girlfriend or buddies at a bar to watch football games. Caleb, for one, had decided he wasn't made for a high-adrenaline lifestyle. He didn't know what motivated Donahue, but both had ultimately made the move to Homicide, where they'd stayed friends of a sort despite the twenty-year difference between them. They hadn't been close enough to really stay in touch after Caleb left KCPD and took the job as sheriff of this rural northeast-Missouri county.

Which made today's phone call a puzzle.

"You're not bored out of your skull yet?" Donahue asked him.

Thinking of his last few wildly busy days, Caleb laughed. "Don't have time to get bored. Do you have any idea how shorthanded a department like mine is? When I'm not juggling too few officers to cover shifts, I'm riding patrol to fill a gap, or giving talks to community organizations. I respond to accidents. My two detectives need guidance. When we have anything halfway serious happen, I usually take lead. I give press conferences, deal with the county commissioners, unhappy citizens. Come to think of it, it's not all that different from heading a homicide squad, except you can keep out of the public eye."

"Good thing, considering my general lack of tact."

With a grin, Caleb said, "Won't disagree." When Donahue didn't make an immediate comeback, Caleb remarked, "Saw on the news that you had a couple of detectives shot a week or so ago. They yours?"

The sergeant gusted a sigh. "Yeah, and that's really why I called. I'm hoping you'll do something for me."

Caleb's eyebrows climbed. Now, this was unexpected. "And what would that be?" he asked, trying to hide his caution.

"Has to do with the shooting." Donahue gave him more detail about the ugly scene in the alley than news outlets had reported. Two young detectives—partners—who'd to all appearances shot each other. One dead, one badly injured but surviving.

"The survivor is a woman," Donahue said grimly. "She came up from patrol not quite a year ago. Seemed to be catching on fine. Detective Walker said he was happy with the pairing. Still, I had a lot of faith in him, and she's new. I think she's corrupt, and murdered him when he found out she was involved in something bad."

"You're thinking drugs?"

"We both know that's the likely answer. They were in the Prospect corridor, behind a bar where we've made more than a few arrests for drugs and prostitution. So far as I can determine, there was no reason they should have been there. I can't find a connection between the bar or nearby businesses and any of the investigations they were conducting."

Caleb frowned. The neighborhood surrounding the intersection of Prospect and Independence ranked as one of the most dangerous areas in Kansas City.

He asked questions; Donahue answered them with seeming frankness. No, he had no concrete evidence that Detective Baker had gone bad.

"I'm going with my gut here," he admitted.

"What's *she* say?"

"She claims amnesia. Can't remember a damn thing. I don't buy it."

"I've seen people with post-traumatic amnesia," Caleb said neutrally.

"This is just too convenient for me."

Inclined to agree with that assessment, Caleb still reserved judgment. It happened, in particular after a head injury, which he understood the woman detective had suffered. He had no trouble understanding Mike Donahue's frustration, though.

He took his feet off the desk so that he could rock forward and reach for his coffee cup. After a swallow, he asked, "So what's this favor?"

"Baker left the hospital yesterday to stay with family to recuperate. Aunt and uncle have a farm in your county. Sam Kirk drove her up there. You remember him, don't you?"

"Mostly by reputation," he said. The guy was a little older than Caleb, solid at his job so far as he knew.

"It's a strange setup, way I hear it. This family is Amish."

Stunned, he said, "What?"

"You heard me. I don't know how Baker is connected to these people. They don't usually want anything to do with law enforcement, from what I understood."

"You understand right. For the most part, they're law-abiding people. They keep to themselves and avoid mixing with government or police authority as much as possible. I've never heard of an Amishman—" and a woman was even more unlikely "—becoming a cop." Caleb shook his head in bemusement. There had to be a story here.

"Not sure she ever was Amish, just somehow related." Donahue cleared his throat. "I'm hoping you'd be willing to stop by, express concern and sympathy. Be good if you could get to know her, sound her out."

"Earn her trust."

"You got it."

The role sounded distasteful to Caleb, but if this woman had really shot her partner in cold blood because she'd taken payoffs to protect drug traffickers, he had no sympathy for her. He couldn't quite see her spilling to him, but people made mistakes. She might forget some detail of whatever story she'd given Donahue, tell Caleb something different. Anything was possible.

"I'll give it a shot," he said, then winced at his choice of words. "Email me everything you've got on the incident. Name and address of this aunt and uncle, too."

His day stayed busy. It wasn't until after dinner at home that he was able to open his laptop and read the police reports and autopsy report Donahue had sent, as promised. Crime scene photos were included. Caleb studied those carefully, but nothing jumped out at him.

Then he saw where Abigail Baker had taken refuge.

Caleb knew Eli and Nancy Kemp. They were good people, Eli a farmer who also worked in leather, making and repairing horse tack, essential to a people whose principal mode of transportation was horse and buggy. Frowning, Caleb tried to find an explanation of why this female cop would have been taken in by an Amishman who also happened to be a minister in his church district.

Nothing.

Abigail was a common name among the Amish, he reflected, but not as much these days among the Englisch, as the Amish labeled most Americans outside their faith.

Caleb sat thinking for a minute. Then he went online again and searched for news coverage of the shooting.

Nothing was materially different from what he'd seen covered on news channels at the time it happened, or what was contained in the information Donahue had sent him. There was a photo of the deceased, Detective Neal Walker. Good-looking fellow listed as thirty-five years old, newly married, a decorated cop.

Could he have been involved with his female partner, then dumped her to maintain his marriage? Say she stewed for a while, then they had it out?

It took him a little longer to find a decent picture of Detective Abigail Baker. Eventually, several popped up. The first was a posed image taken by a professional photographer, Baker dressed in her uniform, looking solemn. And, damn, she was a beautiful woman.

No, he decided after a minute, not exactly that; *pretty* might be a better word, or *cute*. She had a heart-shaped face with a high, wide forehead, a dainty, straight nose and a pretty mouth. Her hair, swept into a sleek arrangement of some kind on the back of her head, was the color of corn silk. Her eyes were sky blue.

Yeah, and he was descending to clichés to describe a lovely woman he didn't want to believe could be accepting payoffs from drug traffickers or the like.

He clicked on a couple of other photos, one taken at the scene of a four-car accident with fatalities, the other of her coming out of the courthouse after testifying in a trial. Both let him see that she had spectacular curves and was tall for a woman, likely five foot ten or so.

Caleb realized he could easily picture her in Amish dress and prayer *kapp*. Eli Kemp was blond and blue-eyed, in fact. Abigail's height would be unusual for an Amishwoman, however.

He went back to the first picture that only displayed her from the shoulders up, mesmerized by eyes he found…haunting. Her lips were shaped into a pleasant smile, but her eyes said something else altogether. She looked sad.

Caleb frowned at the photo for another minute and then closed his laptop. For Pete's sake, he knew better than to read so much into appearances, especially when that person had been caught at a particular moment by a camera. She might have felt queasy, or been worrying about a bill she hadn't paid…or a lover who'd dumped her.

Lucky that maintaining his cop's skepticism came naturally to him. Given his profession, it was a useful skill.

ABBY CLUTCHED THE handrail as she descended the stairs the following morning. She'd slept better than she had in the hospital, in part because of the blessed silence and the true darkness of countryside not brightened by electric lights, and with the moon at a quarter. The moment she'd sat up, dizziness had almost persuaded her to sink back onto her bed. But her aunt and uncle were early risers, and she didn't want to lounge in bed when she ought to be offering to help with daily chores. Still, donning a dress worn without a bra and fastened by straight pins rather than zippers and buttons felt like a huge effort. She managed, but gasped a few times when her healing wounds protested as she stretched too much. And her head… Would it *ever* stop pounding?

Dismayed by how weak she felt, she sat again on the edge of her bed to brush her hair, careful to avoid the still-painful lump, and bundle the mass into a bun she covered with the *kapp*. Of course, she couldn't check her appearance in a mirror; vanity was not encouraged by the Amish, probably why she'd never wasted much time worrying about her looks. In college she'd tried wearing makeup, but felt uncomfortable, not like herself at all, and had thrown it all away.

When she reached the first floor, Aenti Nancy

popped out of the kitchen, exclaiming, "You should have stayed in bed! You have no color in your face." She shook her head. "Ah, well, you're this far. *Komm, komm.* You must have something to eat, feel better then, ain't so?"

Abby trailed her into the kitchen.

"Sit," her aunt ordered. "Tea?"

Abby actually had switched to coffee on an everyday basis, since it was nearly impossible to get a decent cup of tea at the station or a convenience store when she was patrolling, but she always reverted when home.

"Ja," she said in Deitsch, better known as Pennsylvania Dutch even though it was actually a Germanic dialect. *"Denke.* But I can get it…"

Aenti Nancy flapped her apron at her. "It's too soon. You must sit, let us take care of you. So good it is to have you home."

Abby felt her smile wobble. "It is good to be here. I can't thank you enough for taking me in. I didn't know where else to go."

"Always," her aunt said simply, good enough not to ask about Abby's father. "Did Rose tell you she plans to name her girl baby for you?"

"No. Oh, my." An unexpected emotional response sweeping over her, Abby imagined holding a baby girl, her namesake, blinking up at her, her cheeks rosy.

Aenti Nancy set a plate heaped with pancakes in front of her. Within moments, she added butter and syrup as well as a bowl of applesauce and a giant sweet roll, as if Abby could possibly eat so much.

Made-from-scratch pancakes were so much better than anything she got at chain restaurants, and the butter was real, the syrup made from blueberries grown here on the farm. The sweet roll, still warm from the oven, Abby could only call heavenly. Even so, the best she could do was a few bites, earning her a chiding from her aunt.

Sipping tea, she watched her aunt work, dashing between the pantry and the stove, occasionally trotting down to the cellar for jars of fruit or vegetables she'd preserved herself. Since her youngest daughter, Sarah, had married and moved out, Aenti Nancy was alone to cook and manage the house. Of the two sons still at home, one was only sixteen, the other, Isaac, in his early twenties, as yet unmarried.

She did allow Abby to string and snap green beans for the midday meal, and rinse marionberries before they went into a pie. Then she conceded that Abby could step out on the back porch and ring the bell to summon the men.

Onkel Eli, Isaac and lanky, shy Joshua came in the back door, hung their broad-brimmed hats on hooks just inside and went to the sink to wash their hands before sitting down at the long table. Aenti Nancy had what always seemed to Abby to be an enormous midday meal all ready. But Amish men and women alike did hard physical labor almost from the moment they rose in the morning, and needed the calories.

They all bowed their heads in silent prayer before beginning to dish up. Like a swarm of locusts, the men emptied serving dishes piled with mashed potatoes, gravy, green beans and applesauce, while the fried chicken and sourdough biscuits disappeared as fast. Still full from her abundant breakfast, Abby only nibbled. The marionberry pie met the same fate as the rest of the meal.

With a few words of thanks, the men went back to work. Her aunt rejected her offer to help clear the table or wash dishes, suggesting she ought to nap.

"I've been in bed for a week," she protested. "I might go sit out on the porch swing, or lie on the grass in the shade beneath the tree."

Aenti Nancy smiled. "*Ja*, that is a good idea. I remember as a girl seeing many things in the clouds as they floated in the sky. Castles and galloping horses and ships with full sails. All foolishness, but fun."

"Me, too. I haven't done that in a long time." Since she was a child, here at the farm.

Her aunt gave her a speaking look. "Then go."

This early September day had to be in the nineties, but a faint breeze stirred the leaves of the red maple tree rising close enough to the house to shade the front porch for a few hours of the day. Abby lowered herself slowly to the lawn right at the edge of the shade. The grass felt stiff beneath her hands. She brushed it back and forth, enjoying the texture. An apartment dweller now, when had she last sat on the grass? After a minute, she did lie back and gaze up at the canopy of leaves just starting to be tinged with autumn colors.

The sun blazed, and the sky was an arch of blue without a cloud for her to turn into a fantasy castle. Somehow, she didn't mind. Just lying here felt good. Except…her mind kept wanting to nudge at the dark wall separating her from important memories, like a tongue irresistibly drawn to poke at a loose tooth.

She pushed gently at the wall. It didn't so much as quiver. Ran at it and bounced painfully off, leaving her brain feeling bruised.

Wincing, she told herself to quit. The doctor had said her memories would come in their own time.

Aenti would have any number of biblical quotes to chide her for her impatience. In fact, one popped into her head.

This is the day which the Lord hath made; we will rejoice and be glad in it. Psalms 118. That couldn't be more fitting, she decided, relaxing.

The sun began to creep over her. She ought to move. As fair-skinned as she was, she'd burn. But the heat had made her sleepy. She drifted, aware of distant voices, where her uncle and cousins worked, the bang of the screen on the back door closing once, the darting movement of a squirrel scuttling up the maple. Birds calling, and was that the buzz of a cicada? Her eyelids sank closed.

The sound of an approaching car, its throaty engine and the crunch of gravel beneath its tires, disrupted the utter peace of the afternoon. Abby pried open her eyes and rolled her head on the grass to see the long drive-way. It wasn't as if cars didn't sometimes come down this road. Amish had Englisch friends, or at least ac-quaintances. Customers for their businesses. During their *rumspringa*, or running-around time, teenagers could take advantage of the freedom to ride in cars, and even use cell phones. This might be a friend of Joshua's.

It was actually a big, black SUV that turned into the Kemp driveway. Too large and expensive for any teenager to be driving, surely. Abby sat up, then wished she hadn't. She'd rather be unnoticed by this visitor. Left to her peace.

But instead of proceeding toward the huge, German-style barn, as the driver would have if he'd had business with her uncle, the SUV stopped closest to the house. A man got out on the far side of it and walked around to the front bumper.

A police officer, she saw with a jolt, tall, well built, his hair brown. He wore dark glasses, but she'd swear he was looking straight at her.

He turned, then, though, and she saw that Onkel Eli was coming from the barn to meet this man. The screen door rattled, and she suspected that her aunt was sneaking a peek out, too, to see who was here. Having a law-enforcement officer show up, that couldn't be a common occurrence. Well, besides her.

Her uncle and the stranger spoke briefly as she watched. Surely Onkel Eli would answer his ques-tions and he'd go away.

But, no. They both turned to look at her now, then

walked toward her. Inexplicably disturbed, Abby saw that the cop was a head taller than her uncle, broad shouldered, and moved with a confident, purposeful stride. The short sleeves of the moss green uniform shirt exposed strong brown forearms dusted with hair bleached almost blond. As he approached, she realized he had to be six foot four or taller. And she was a little bit embarrassed to notice what large hands he had, too.

She ought to get up, she realized, but knew the process would be awkward. She hated the idea of being on her hands and knees in front of this man. So she stayed put, squinting against the sun as she gazed up at them.

"Onkel?"

"*Ja*, niece, this is Sheriff Caleb Tanner. He has come to see you."

"To see me?" How strange.

"That's right." The sheriff crouched to be closer to her level, the fabric of his black uniform trousers pulling tight over powerful muscles. Resting an elbow on his thigh, he held out the other hand to her.

Feeling reluctant, she let him engulf and gently squeeze her hand.

"I'm sure Sheriff Tanner would like a cup of coffee and a slice of your *aenti*'s *schnitz* pie, *ja*?"

It almost sounded good, despite the nausea that returned unpredictably. Abby knew her aunt and uncle were dismayed by her scant appetite.

The sheriff smiled, momentarily brightening

hazel eyes. He extended his hand again. "Let me help you up?"

She hesitated, but finally mumbled, "Thank you," and once again felt his grip close around her fingers. As he rose, he easily pulled her to her feet. She ended up disturbingly close to his big body and took a hasty step back. Her cheeks burned, and she tried to convince herself she'd gotten too much sun.

The three of them walked in together, using the front door because it was closest. Or perhaps because the sheriff was, if not a stranger to her aunt and uncle, an *auslander*, an outsider, for sure. Family and friends used the back door.

Abby would have hurried if she could, knowing what a mess she must be. *Strubly*, in Deitsch. *Disheveled*. Her apron was askew, hair tumbling out of the bun, and when she lifted a hand to her head, she realized her *kapp* had slid back. Then, of course, she must have bits of grass in her hair and on her skirts.

Once inside, she mumbled, "Excuse me for a minute," and hustled for the downstairs bathroom. A small mirror hung there, allowing members of the household to check to be sure their hair was smooth, or *kapps* and bonnets in the proper position. Indeed, she had to pick blades of grass out of her hair, which she finger-combed and reanchored before settling the filmy white *kapp* back on her head, leaving the ties dangling. She made a face at herself, dismayed by still pink cheeks.

By the time she reached the kitchen, Onkel Eli

and the sheriff were both digging into huge pieces of *schnitz* pie, made from dried apples. The sheriff paused when he saw her, a forkful halfway to his mouth. His eyes narrowed slightly as his gaze swept over her, head to foot and back up again, bringing renewed warmth to her cheeks.

Her aunt spoke to her in Deitsch. "Sit, Abby. You must eat, too. Hot water I have on for tea. Eat yourself full, and no nonsense about you not being hungry. You hear me?" She slid a plate in front of Abby as she sat beside Onkel Eli.

"I hear you," Abby said meekly, in English.

Sheriff Tanner looked amused. Had he understood the Deitsch? Abby wondered.

"Your sergeant called me," he said. "Asked me to make sure you're doing okay. He was worried that they'd let you out of the hospital too soon."

"With family, she's better off," Aenti said fiercely.

"Yes, I have no doubt."

This smile for her aunt transformed an astonishingly handsome face that had first seemed grim to Abby. He had high cheekbones, a strong jaw already showing a hint of brown stubble, a thin nose that might have a tiny crook, as if it had been broken at some time, and a mouth Abby had trouble taking her eyes from.

"Who wouldn't rather lie in the sun than a hospital bed?" he added.

"It did feel good," Abby admitted. She took a small bite, seeing Aenti Nancy's nod of satisfaction.

Once she'd chewed and swallowed, Abby met his eyes. "How did Sergeant Donahue choose you?" If he heard some sharpness, she didn't care.

"We knew each other years ago. I was with KCPD before I became sheriff here. Mike is sure I must be bored."

"Maybe he's right, if you had enough time on your hands to drive out here to see whether I was in dire straits or up and walking."

Her uncle's eyebrows rose, but he didn't say anything. The sheriff's twitched, too.

"I like to get out and drive around my county," he said mildly. "Say hello to people. Haven't spoken to Eli in a while."

That might all be true. Abby didn't even know why she was bristling. And being rude.

No, she knew, all right. She'd reacted to him instantly in a way she never had to any man. It made her uncomfortable. She didn't really know how to flirt, and shouldn't anyway in case he was married. Or, even more likely, not attracted to her. And then there was the idea that Sergeant Donahue had sent him. The sergeant she'd trusted, who'd stood at the foot of her hospital bed looking at her with suspicion and something stronger. Dislike? Anger? And suddenly now he'd become considerate, deeply concerned about her well-being? Abby didn't think so.

Caleb Tanner drained his coffee. She saw that he'd finished his pie, too.

So she said politely, "Thank you for coming. You

can tell him I'm fine, but no, I haven't remembered anything."

He studied her with eyes that she decided were a very dark green flecked with gold and possibly whiskey brown. With a nod, he said, "I'll tell him."

He thanked Aenti Nancy for the pie, said a general goodbye and walked out, Onkel Eli accompanying him.

Abby sagged and closed her eyes.

Chapter Three

Three days later, Caleb thought of an errand that would provide him with an adequate excuse to be in Eli Kemp's neighborhood so that he could reasonably stop by again. He felt certain Abigail Baker—Abby, her aunt had called her—would not be thrilled to see him again. Because she had secrets? Or suspected his motives?

One thing he knew: she wasn't fine. As he'd tugged her to her feet the other day and then when she walked to the house slowly, pain had tightened a face that was already drawn and too pale—except when she'd blushed. Caleb doubted the bruised circles beneath her eyes were usual for her, either. Was she having difficulty sleeping? Guilt could do that—but so could trauma. Even if she'd truly lost all memory of what happened, she *had* seen her partner go down. The subconscious was powerful. He'd bet money she was having nightmares when she did sleep. If he could get her to talk about the nightmares…

And what were the odds of that? She hadn't exactly been grateful he'd come by, or seen the possibility of a new friend in him. He grimaced. Apparently, he'd have to be more charming. Maybe steer away from asking about the shooting for now, unless she raised the subject.

He turned into the driveway, which was really two dirt ruts with a hillock of grass between them. At the sight of the big white farmhouse ahead, his stomach growled. It occurred to him that there'd be a substantial culinary benefit to courting Abby Baker's trust.

Once again, he parked close to the house. Eli stuck his head out of the barn, but Caleb waved him off and went to the front door. Nancy let him in with a big smile, expressing in her strongly accented English her delight at seeing him again.

Then she lowered her voice. "Good for Abby, seeing you will be." A hint of worry crossed her face. "Do you understand Deitsch?"

"Ja," he said, switching languages. "I had many Amish friends as a boy."

"Gut, gut!" Her smile didn't return, however, and she was almost whispering. "Abby is feeling low, I think. I tell her she must trust in God, and try, she does, but…" She shook her head sadly.

"She's depressed," he said in English, not sure of the word in Deitsch.

Nancy sounded out the word, looking uncertain. "Where is she?"

She straightened and assumed the smile that he

imagined was her usual expression. "The kitchen. Today, we bake."

Caleb hoped Abby wasn't helping too much. Even aside from the consequences of her concussion, she'd been seriously wounded less than two weeks ago.

He followed Nancy inside.

"Who's here?" Abby asked, then saw him when he stepped into the kitchen. Some emotion flared in her blue eyes before she shut the door on whatever she'd been thinking.

Caleb was reminded that she was a cop, not a sweet-natured Amish *maidal* who'd never learned to veil her thoughts.

"Abigail," he said with a nod. "Or do you prefer Abby?"

Her hesitation was brief. "Abby. I didn't expect to see you again so soon, Sheriff."

"Caleb."

Despite clear reluctance, she nodded acceptance. "Caleb."

At Nancy's urging, he sat across from Abby, who had been shaping dough into balls she set on cookie sheets and then gently flattened with the bottom of a canning jar. For a fleeting instant, he imagined her hand competently holding a nine-millimeter gun. Cookies and guns didn't go together.

Despite the photos of Abigail he'd seen online, here and now she looked Amish. An Amishwoman brandishing a handgun? Never.

Her aunt brought him a cup of coffee and an enormous wedge of marionberry pie topped with ice cream. He thanked her and dug in. For the first time, Caleb saw a spark of amusement on Abby's face.

"Now I know why you're here."

He grinned. "When I pulled in, I was thinking I'd better put in some extra time on the treadmill if I plan to stop. No way I'm turning down one of Nancy's desserts."

"Denke," her aunt said over her shoulder. "Abby helped with the pie, ain't so?"

Abby chuckled. "I rolled out the crust. I'll take credit for that much."

She continued with the cookies, her hands quick and sure. Every so often, she glanced at him, her expression one of perplexity, if he was reading her right. Finally, she asked, "Did you report to Sergeant Donahue that you'd done your duty?"

He took a long swallow of coffee. "I did. I assured him you seemed to be on the road to recovery but haven't remembered anything, just as you told me." He frowned. "A concussion that can cause partial amnesia is a bad one. Are you still having headaches?"

"Yes, unfortunately. *Headaches* plural isn't quite the right word. My headache doesn't come and go," she said wryly. "It just stays."

"Seriously?" He pushed his empty plate aside.

"Seriously. I have pills, but they make me sleepy and foggy. I don't like the feeling."

"You like having a chronic headache?"

She wrinkled her nose, for a second looking like a teenager. "You know the saying, 'Between the devil and the deep blue sea.'"

Out of the corner of his eye, Caleb saw her aunt watching them, crinkled lines of perturbation between her eyebrows.

"I understand," he said gently. "I was in a bad car accident a few years back." He'd been part of a vehicle pursuit, unaware the driver they were chasing had circled back until he burst from a side street and smashed into the driver's side of Caleb's patrol car at full speed. "Recovery and rehab took almost three months." His hip still hurt fiercely when he overdid it.

"Really?" Those astonishing blue eyes searched his, as if she needed to know he was sincere, that he truly understood what she was going through.

"Really."

"I'm lucky I only have the one cracked bone," she said thoughtfully, likely not aware that she'd laid a hand over her chest. "They're slower to heal than soft tissue."

"I can speak to that." He rubbed his hip without thinking. "The trouble is, with broken bones you lose a lot of muscle tone before you can start physical therapy." Caleb frowned again. "Shouldn't you be having therapy?"

"I started in the hospital, and came with a long list of exercises. The therapist would like me to check in weekly with him, but I'd need to hire a car and driver or take the bus. He said I could find someone local instead."

"I'd drive you to Kansas City," Caleb heard himself say.

Nancy smiled at him. "What a kind suggestion!"

Abby was slower to respond, instead studying him again, as if trying to see a lot deeper than he'd like. "Why would you do that?" she said finally, but without the underlying hostility he'd heard at his last visit.

"This has been rough on you." And it would give him lots of time to earn her trust, encourage confidence. "I spent twelve years with KCPD, which means we ought to be able to rely on each other." That, he decided, was actually honest.

She nodded after a minute. She had a habit of taking her time before committing to anything, Caleb realized.

"If you can drive me this week, that would be good. Gerald, my physical therapist, can tell best if I'm progressing. If he thinks I'm doing well, it would make sense for me to find someone here after that."

"Make an appointment and let me know when. Ah…can you? Did you bring your phone or computer?"

"No," she said softly. "But I have the number and can call from the phone shanty."

"Or do you want to use my phone and do it now?"

"I'd rather finish this." She lifted flour-covered hands.

"You'll call me, too?"

"*Ja*, you, too." This sounded impish.

"Then let me give you my number." He pulled card and pen from his vest pocket and jotted down his mobile phone number, then slid it across the table to Abby. "I don't have any set appointments this week—" actually, he did, but would change them for this "—so any time is good."

"Thank you." She looked at him with an openness and warmth that hit him like a blow. "Aenti Nancy is right. Your offer is kind."

Leaving, he told himself he'd been smacked with guilt, that's all…but he knew better than to lie to himself. Abby Baker might not have the finely carved face of a model, but in his eyes she was beautiful. Especially at that moment.

After getting in his department SUV, he sat for a minute, unmoving, gazing toward the house.

He couldn't let himself get sucked in. Donahue wouldn't have asked him to do this if he hadn't had good reason for his suspicion. Caleb knew the man. Caleb didn't know Detective Abigail Baker, and wasn't fool enough to let a pretty face and bright blue eyes divert him from keeping his promise.

Besides, if he could confirm her innocence, he'd be doing *her* a favor.

He started the engine, lifted a hand toward a young man who was peering out from between open barn doors, and swung in a U-turn to go back to town, and the pile of work awaiting him.

A GUN BLASTED. Once, twice.

She managed to fumble a hand toward her un-snapped holster. Why was it empty? She was peering at the dark bulk of someone crouching over—puzzlement. She ought to know who lay there, not so far from her.

She hovered on the edge of darkness. When the footsteps approached, it took everything she had to open her eyes a slit. The toe of the boots came to a stop inches from her. He must be looking down at her.

A voice calling from a distance.

Crack. *She jerked, and pain exploded in her chest.*

I'm dead, she realized.

But she couldn't be, because hands were shaking her.

"Abby!" the woman exclaimed. "Abby? *Was is letz?*" *What is wrong?*

The nightmare faded out of sight, leaving only dread and shock. Abby forced her eyes open and pushed herself to a sitting position, her wounds protesting. "Aenti Nancy?"

"*Ja*. Oh, child." Warm, comforting arms came around her. "You cried out, as if—"

"It was a nightmare." She sagged. "Just a nightmare." Even if she'd been able to remember it, the mind twisted real events in a dreamscape. She couldn't rely on whatever she saw in a nightmare.

Aenti Nancy insisted on bringing her a cupful of

warm milk to help her sleep. Weirdly, the idea was comforting. Grossmammi had warmed milk for her when she was a child with insomnia or after a nightmare. Abby didn't love the taste, but she would drink it anyway, and gratefully.

Once she had, and had persuaded her aunt that she could go back to sleep now, Abby lay gazing toward the uncovered window, where she could see a crescent moon.

This would be a big day. The sheriff was to pick her up at nine in the morning to drive her to her appointment in Kansas City. She had to squelch any sense of anticipation. He might have offered only so as to look good in her aunt's and uncle's eyes, and thereby the view of all the Amish in their church district. Abby imagined Aenti nodding firmly to her friends and saying, "The sheriff is Englisch, but a *gut* man." The others would take that in and decide that if they had to have dealings with authorities, he at least might be trustworthy.

Of course, there was also the distinct possibility that he intended to worm his way into her confidence so that she'd tell him everything that happened in that alley. If Sergeant Donahue hadn't believed in her memory loss, why would the sheriff? Testing her, that's what he was doing, she decided.

He might actually *be* a good man, but not one she could trust. Not yet. Not until she did remember.

Once in a while, she thought she did. Only shreds. Footsteps. The press of dirty asphalt on her cheek.

She might think she smelled something rancid, but then it was gone. Abby had no intention of telling anyone that even such meaningless pieces seemed to float to the surface occasionally. The doctor had told her not to try to force memories, that it wouldn't do any good, that her mind needed to heal.

Onkel Eli had checked messages at the shanty this afternoon, too, and found three for her. Two were from other detectives, wanting to know how she was. The third had been left by Sergeant Donahue, who asked that she call.

She wished he hadn't given out her number to the others. They might be able to find where she was, with the phone number as a starting point.

No, wait. Sam Kirk had the address, too, so it wasn't exactly a secret. Anyway, she was here to recover, not to hide.

Except… Abby couldn't forget that *somebody* had tried to kill her, and she didn't believe for a minute that it had been Neal. Someone else had to have been there.

She concentrated, but not so much as a flicker of memory materialized out of the night.

She remained restless enough to be glad when the window framed the pearly gray of dawn. Abby watched as the sky slowly brightened, waiting until she heard footsteps in the hall, first soft ones, then firmer, booted steps. As tired as she was, her lips curved; Joshua would have a hard time dragging himself out of bed this morning. She'd heard him come in late last night, trying to be quiet, but he'd bumped the wall twice. He'd likely been drinking, which wouldn't make his parents happy, even if it was common with kids during *rumspringa*. One of Abby's cousins had done worse than that. Ruth had gotten pregnant. Of course her come-calling friend had married her, after both had gone through counseling with the bishop and sworn repentance before the congregation. Ruth and Aaron had four children now and were expecting another, according to Aenti Nancy. They had moved farther south for affordable land, but visited once or twice a year.

Abby got dressed, the motions practiced. With each passing day, she walked better, but still had to take the stairs with extra care. Isaac reached the kitchen only moments after she did, his relief obvious when he saw that the coffee was ready. Abby took over making the scrambled eggs while Aenti cut up and fried potatoes and toasted bread in the oven. Refrigerator and stove were powered by gas. Many of the smaller appliances, like Aenti's prized food processor, were hand cranked and did the job splendidly.

Onkel Eli sent Isaac back upstairs to wake his brother, who trailed down ten minutes later, eyelids heavy, hair poking every which way. His father scrutinized him, but said nothing. Breakfast was usually a quiet meal, the men eager to eat and get out to work. Abby felt a little queasy again, and had only eggs and a single piece of toast. She had to be

losing weight, which wasn't a bad thing, whatever
Aenti said to the contrary. Out in the world, slender
figures were admired, not too-tall women with too-
generous curves.

Despite her tiredness, she cleared the table and
washed the dishes, too, while Aenti dried. Her in-
defatigable aunt planned to do some canning, but
Abby admitted to needing to sit down. Shooed out
onto the front porch, she settled on a rocker and set
it into gentle motion.

CALEB GLANCED SIDELONG at Abby, who still looked
befuddled. Or, as the Amish would say, *ferhoodled*.
When he'd arrived, he had spotted her immediately,
sound asleep in a rocking chair on the porch. Her
head had hung at an awkward angle, and now she
occasionally rubbed her neck, as if it was stiff. He
knew she'd been embarrassed to be caught unawares.

Cop, he thought again. Of course she was disturbed to discover anyone at all could have walked
right up to her while she dozed. For Abby, the bone-
deep dislike of being vulnerable must be cranked up
tenfold, given that she'd lost her partner and been
shot herself so recently, with no idea who her enemy
was.

Unless she knew exactly what had happened.

He cleared his throat. "Did you have trouble sleeping last night?"

She studied his profile in her serious way. "Yes,"

she said at last. "I had a nightmare and then couldn't get back to sleep."

"About the shooting?"

"I…don't know."

Hearing reservation in her voice, he gave her a sideways look. "It probably was. I deal with things I've seen and done on the job pretty well during the day, but corralling my sleeping mind is another story."

"That's true. As I wake up, I think I'll remember, but then it's just gone. It's really frustrating." She frowned, looking ahead through the windshield at the rolling, forested country they were passing through. "Although I can't trust that a nightmare was truthful."

"Probably not," Caleb agreed, "but there might be a nugget in there that would start a cascade of memories. In fact, if you *are* dreaming about the shooting, I'd guess it's probably because your memory is starting to break through. Did you have nightmares at first?"

The creases on her forehead deepened. "No. They had me pretty doped up, though."

"That doesn't do much for clarity of thinking, does it?"

She smiled wryly. "No."

Which was why she had a headache bad enough he could see it, like a dark aura.

"I wonder if massage would help your headaches. *Headache,*" he amended.

"Don't know. My neck, now…" Abby kneaded it again with her right hand.

He itched to take over the task, suspecting her skin would feel like pure silk beneath his fingertips.

"Why aren't you tanned?" he asked, probably too abruptly.

Obviously startled, she said after a pause, "I just don't. I use a lot of sunscreen, because otherwise I burn. I should probably move to the Pacific Northwest, where the skies are gray a good percent of the time."

He laughed. "Your nose is a little pink."

Abby sighed. "And I've been trying to stay in the shade."

Conversation wandered, with Caleb forgetting for stretches what his real purpose was here. Eventually, Abby asked about his decision to leave the Kansas City PD to become the sheriff of a rural county.

"Each promotion meant more time spent doing admin. As a lieutenant, I traded off getting out in the field with having more control over decisions that impacted the officers beneath me." He grimaced. "Or so I thought. After a while, I realized I felt as if I was being ground between two big rocks."

"The *mano* and the *metate*," Abby murmured.

"What?"

"That's what the Mayans and Aztecs and a lot of the Southwest Native Americans used to grind corn. When I was a kid, my parents took me to New Mexico, and I saw a Navajo woman using a *mano* and the *metate*." She mimed the action, then shrugged. "It was interesting."

Intrigued, he looked at her a little too long and had to jerk his attention back to the road.

"That was me. A kernel of corn. I heard the sheriff here in Hearn County had to step down because of health problems, and I liked the idea of complete control." His mouth curved. "Goes without saying that was a fantasy. I let myself forget the county commissioners, outraged citizens, news reporters…" He exaggerated his disgruntlement. "Somebody is always mad about something."

Her chuckle was a happy sound that had him stealing another too-long glance. "Not a lot of exciting investigations, either, I bet."

"In the sense of a puzzle, no." Until she'd come along. "I'm finding I like the challenges, though. Dealing with the Amish, not to mention the tourists, being a politician, improving training for my deputies, juggling to fill shifts and have people where they need to be." His shoulders moved. "And I'm home."

She asked about that, too, and he told a few stories about growing up in a rambling old house on acreage just outside Ruston with his brother and sister, being free to roam the woods up behind the house, ride his bike to friends', fish in the pond and creek. "I like the pace here," he finished.

"I do, too," she admitted, sounding subdued. Or was that sad?

"If you don't mind my asking, how'd you end up with Amish relatives?"

"My mother left the faith to marry my father." That much she said matter-of-factly. "She hadn't been baptized yet, so she was able to visit. I loved spending time on the farm, which belonged to my grandparents then. Onkel Eli took over after Grossdaadi died."

Since the Amish were a sect of the Anabaptists, they didn't believe in infant baptism. In their view, each individual was baptized upon accepting the faith—which was usually in the late teens or early twenties. Caleb nodded his understanding and asked, "Your grandmother?"

"She only lived two years after he was gone. I wasn't around much, which I regret, but when I saw her, I had the feeling she was tired. She missed him."

Caleb could see that happening to his parents, who had a spark and a friendship that he didn't often see in couples married as long as they'd been. Maybe he couldn't solely blame his job for the failure of his two or three more serious relationships. He had wanted what his parents had, and not found it.

"What about your parents?" he asked.

"My mother died when I was a child," she said calmly. "I spent a lot of time here after that. Oh," she said, in what he had no trouble recognizing as a diversion, "I didn't tell you what exit to take, did I?"

Interesting. Caleb felt sure a story lay behind her few words, but it wasn't one she was ready to tell him. He wondered if she ever talked about her childhood. Some instinct said no. Yeah, and while he was wondering, he was struck anew by her decision to become a cop despite what had to have been a serious dose of Amish values.

The Amish had been persecuted and even burned alive in the old country, and had determined in North America to stay apart, to avoid being influenced by the wider culture—and to submit as little as possible to government authority. They believed in forgiveness rather than vengeance. Among themselves, if a man repented, he was accepted wholeheartedly back into the fold. Conviction at trial and prison terms were measures they occasionally upheld only in the belief that a man who had stumbled from the path of goodness might be given time to regret his sins and do penance.

Amish did not become law-enforcement officers. So what had motivated Abby Baker?

One more answer he wouldn't get today.

They'd wandered into discussing the health-care system by the time he parked in the lot outside the medical building that housed her physical therapist. When she quit talking midsentence, Caleb followed her gaze to see an unmarked police car two slots away. Sergeant Michael Donahue climbed out, his eyes on Abby.

Irked, Caleb wondered why he was here, and without issuing a warning.

Chapter Four

Sergeant Donahue stood with his feet planted apart, blocking her way on the sidewalk in front of the clinic. His arms were crossed and his eyes lingered either on her face or the filmy white *kapp* covering her hair, she couldn't decide.

Abby was slow enough to move; Caleb had gotten all the way around to her side and opened the door. He helped her out of his car and kept a hand beneath her elbow. Whether he intended to support her physically or emotionally she had no idea. Or was any support at all only a pretense? She didn't shake him off, because her headache pulsed at the mere sight of the hard suspicion in Donahue's eyes.

"Sergeant," she said stiffly. Furious because she knew her cheeks were reddening, she dipped her head. "If you don't mind, I need to check in."

Donahue didn't bother with a greeting. "What in hell is that getup?"

Her chin tipped up. "I dress plain when I stay with my Amish family," she said, praying she could maintain her dignity. "I'm sure Detective Kirk told you about my aunt and uncle."

His lip curled. "He didn't say you'd be trying to blend in."

How could this man look at her with such dislike? He *knew* her. At least she'd believed he did. She was only grateful that Caleb hadn't leaped to defend her. Or, come to think of it, to greet his old friend.

Because they planned this confrontation, a voice murmured in her head. How else would the sergeant have known the date and time of her appointment?

She ordered herself to think about that later. She'd have plenty of time during the return drive to tell Sheriff Tanner what she thought of him.

"I spent a great deal of time with my mother's family growing up. This—" she plucked at her calf-length dress and apron "—feels as natural to me as my uniform. Now, if you'll excuse me…"

He still didn't back out of her way. "I'm waiting for answers, Detective Baker. Don't think you can hide from me."

Abby kept her chin up and refused to look away first. After a minute, his gaze flicked to the sheriff beyond her shoulder. Then he stepped aside and swept an arm out in a courtly gesture that mocked her. She walked past him and kept going, not so much as glancing back.

Caleb took a few steps with her, murmuring in her ear, "I'll be right in. Let me talk to him for a minute."

"Of course you want to talk to him," she said acidly, not looking to see how he reacted.

The receptionist inside appeared startled by her garb, but didn't remark. The Amish didn't like big cities, so the woman might never have seen an Amish person unless she'd spent a weekend sightseeing in Amish country, where most who visited would squeal with delight at spotting a horse-drawn black buggy on the road or a vegetable stand overseen by women in their distinctive dresses, aprons and *kapps*.

A part of Abby wished she'd brought her Englisch clothes and asked Caleb to stop at a service station so she could go into the restroom and change. Another part refused to feel embarrassed. Certainly, she wasn't ashamed. This was her, as much as the cop was.

And *that* was something Sergeant Donahue hadn't known about her.

CALEB GLARED AT DONAHUE. "What are you doing here?"

"Figured she was due for a little reminder."

"You've just undermined any progress I made with her. Now she thinks I set this up."

A dark eyebrow lifted. "Didn't you?"

"I gave you an update." Caleb's voice rose. "I thought you had the brains not to blow it!"

"Don't tell me that sweet face has gotten to you," the other man said contemptuously.

Caleb took a step forward, letting the jackass

know how aggressive he felt. He reveled in the advantage his greater height gave him. "You're the one who set this up. You want me to drop her at home and forget about it?"

Donahue's jaw muscles knotted. "No."

"Then make an effort not to sabotage me."

A lot angrier than was probably justified, Caleb stalked toward the entrance of the physical-therapy clinic, much like Abby had.

A quick scan didn't find her in the waiting area, although several people were there slouching in chairs, either staring blankly at a big television screen tuned to a twenty-four-hour news station or flipping idly through magazines. When the receptionist asked brightly if she could help him, he shook his head.

"I'm waiting for Ms. Baker."

He took a seat where he could see everyone else in the room as well as the front entrance and the door that led to the back. He let his gaze flick to the television—and the latest political squabble—then back to the glass doors. There was no reason for him to feel so on edge. Abby wasn't in any danger at the moment, nor could he use this time to learn anything more about her. But he didn't relax well in the midst of strangers, and it took him a few minutes to understand that he'd been offended when that idiot Donahue looked at her the way he had only because of the clothes she wore.

To use Amish parlance, Caleb was a *modern*,

through and through. Even if he'd shared their faith, he was incapable of what they called *gelassenheit*. The concept meant yielding oneself to the will of God and to the church in the form of the bishop and ministers. Caleb had never been good at yielding himself to anyone's authority, which explained his decision to take the job as sheriff. He'd seen for himself that the Amish acceptance of God's will gave them a peace he'd never find, any more than other moderns would. Most Americans were too competitive, their lives too taken up with striving for more success, more respect, more money.

And yet, he thought he'd learned from his Amish friends as a boy, if only a tolerance that they might call *forgiveness*. He admired much about the Leit—the people, as they called themselves—liked many of the individuals he'd gotten to know. Mike Donahue dropped a few notches in Caleb's esteem for his seeming disdain for a good people.

He frowned, wondering how much Abby had learned from her Amish family. She spoke Deitsch fluently, so she had to have spent substantial time with them. And yet, she'd become a cop.

Maybe on the way home, he could get her to open up to him.

THREE DAYS LATER, Abby was alone in the kitchen, shaping dough to go into greased bread pans, when she heard an unfamiliar engine out front. She groaned. Now who? And why had her fellow officers all taken it into their heads to visit at the same time?

The first she'd appreciated. Julie Luong and Abby had gone through the academy together and been lucky enough to be assigned as rookies to the same precinct. In an environment dominated by men, Abby had been grateful to have a friend she knew wouldn't betray her confidence and who was having a lot of the same experiences she was, good and bad.

Julie initially had looked startled when she saw Abby in Amish garb, and then Onkel Eli with his broad-brimmed hat, clean-shaven upper lip and long beard, but she'd been accepting enough to be warm and friendly when she joined the family for lunch. Before she left, she hugged Abby carefully and whispered, "Please come back. I miss you."

Abby had felt a little emotional.

In contrast, she didn't feel at all weepy after the next day's visitor, a detective from her unit who had laughed raucously when he saw her. Aenti Nancy had been excited that another friend had come to visit and started dishing up pie even before Abby answered the door, but ended up disappointed when she didn't even invite him in. Instead, she told him she didn't feel well and needed to lie down.

She could tell he didn't believe her, but he did leave.

Of course, the sheriff had stopped by daily, sometimes just to say hello, other times lingering for coffee, a piece of pie and conversation with whomever was willing to talk to him.

Which did not include her.

On the drive back from Kansas City the day of her appointment, he'd tried to grill her about her background. Well, he disguised it as conversation, but she knew what he really had in mind. Her aunt and uncle might like this man, but she didn't. She wouldn't relax her guard so quickly again.

That she responded to him on a physical level was something she did her best to hide. Abby didn't even like admitting to herself that her heart stumbled every time she saw him, then sped up. That when he smiled or touched her she felt an unfamiliar, honeyed warmth in her belly and lower.

She'd get over these feelings, she told herself every day after he left. How could she be attracted to a man who believed she was capable of killing her own partner? A man who was only being nice to her because he thought he could lull her into a full confession before he slapped on the cuffs?

The engine she heard now had the throaty roar of a pickup truck or SUV, but she felt sure it wasn't the sheriff's department vehicle.

She took a minute to set the bread pans in the oven to rise again, a cloth laid over them, before she went to peek out the window beside the front door.

Two more detectives from her unit walked toward the porch. She ought to be glad to see them. Hadn't she thought of her fellow officers as family? Until this moment, she hadn't realized how much the sergeant had tainted her feelings. Yesterday's visitor hadn't helped, either.

She wished she weren't alone, but Onkel Eli and Aenti Nancy had left after lunch to visit Rose. Abby had been tempted to go along but was afraid the jolting ride in a buggy would be more than her perpetually aching head could bear. The pain in her sternum wasn't receding as fast as she'd hoped, either. Isaac and Joshua were working out in the field this afternoon and would assume she could handle visitors.

Annoyed with herself, she thought, *Of course I can.* Anyway, if they, too, were going to be jerks, she'd prefer none of her real family were present to see.

Of the two men, she liked Ron Caldwell the best. He'd always teased her as if she was a little sister, and had been helpful when she had questions. His partner, Jason McCarthy, was also big on jokes, but they were cruder, even sometimes seeming mean. He'd sized her up a few times in a way that made her uncomfortable, too, although he'd never asked her out or touched her inappropriately.

Resigning herself, she opened the front door before they'd gotten far enough to knock. "Ron. Jason. I'm surprised to see you."

Ron trailed, his foot on the first step, while Jason was ahead of him. Both stopped dead and stared at her. Of course, it was Jason who let out a whoop of laughter.

When he could control himself, he started to sing. "Mary had a little lamb, little lamb, little lamb. Mary had a—"

She interrupted without compunction. Tersely. "Not funny."

Behind him, Ron was grinning.

"Yeah, it is." Jason turned to his partner and buddy. "Tell her it's funny."

"It's funny," Ron agreed.

Jason let out a hoot. "Man, I didn't believe Donahue, but he was right. This was worth the drive. You look like—I don't even know what. It's like a historical reenactment."

She heard footsteps behind her.

"Abby?" It was Joshua, sounding puzzled. In Deitsch, he said, "Who are these men? What's so funny?"

"These are men I work with in Kansas City. Police officers." She switched to English. "Detective Caldwell and Detective McCarthy, this is my cousin, Joshua Kemp."

Jason's grin widened.

Joshua's expression froze, even as the fiery red color of humiliation rose from beneath his shirt collar and spread to his face. He recognized that he was being mocked. It wouldn't be the first time. Amish had learned to hold up their heads and ignore the ignorant who made fun of them. Unfortunately, what teenager had real confidence?

She'd just never expected men she'd worked with and respected to be among those ignorant.

Jason smirked. "Do you go out in public dressed like this, Detective Baker? Maybe pin your badge to your apron?"

Ron, she knew with one part of her mind, was staying quiet. But he wasn't telling his partner to shut up, either.

A black SUV slammed to a stop behind the pickup the two detectives had driven. Wonderful. Would Sheriff Tanner appreciate the jokes?

At last, her temper sparked along with her headache. "Enough. You're an intolerant boor."

Jason's eyes narrowed. He took a step closer to her, his expression ugly. "You can't take a joke?"

Joshua remained silent behind her, but he was brave enough not to have fled.

"Or is the outfit supposed to convince all of us that you're an angel, that you couldn't possibly have gunned Neal down?"

His scathing tone stung, but she met his glare with her own. "You need to—"

A deep voice came from behind. "It's time for you to go. *Now.*"

Both men whipped around. Neither had noticed the new arrival until he spoke, which should have shocked them. Cops needed to stay aware.

"This isn't your business—" Belatedly, Jason took in the uniform and the star pinned to Caleb's chest pocket.

Caleb's gaze touched hers fleetingly, but long enough for her to see how angry he was.

Ron was smart enough to say, "Jason, get going."

"She didn't even let us in."

"You're invited to visit my jail." Now Caleb's eyes stayed on Jason. "I'm sure your sergeant would be pleased to come up to bail you out."

"I'm not breaking any law," the detective said sullenly. "I work with Abby, and all we did was come to see how she's doing."

"Is that what you were doing?" she asked. "Funny, your visit felt more like an assault than a friendly hello."

Caleb met her eyes again. "How about I arrest them for trespassing?"

She looked at Ron. "Just go, and don't come back."

His face was flushed now. "He really was just kidding around, Abby. But we're going." He turned, hesitated, then brushed by Caleb, who didn't step aside. "Come on, Jason."

Under Caleb's stony stare, Jason apparently lost his nerve and backed away from the doorway. She knew he was a dedicated weight lifter, but somehow his showy muscles didn't look all that impressive next to a man as large and solid as Caleb Tanner. He sidled past, then hurried across the grass toward the pickup truck.

No, he *scuttled*, she decided with satisfaction. Much better choice of words.

All three of them watched until the truck did a

U-turn in front of the barn and disappeared down the driveway. Dust arose on the road a moment later.

"I was capable of getting rid of them without threats," she heard herself say.

Caleb's dark brows rose. "But I enjoyed threatening them."

A laugh burst out of her. She clapped her hand over her mouth but failed to hold back what were really giggles.

"Abby?" Joshua said anxiously. "Abby, are you all right?"

In contrast, Caleb didn't try to hide his amusement. The skin beside his eyes crinkled, and his teeth flashed in a grin.

"Oh, my" were the first words she managed to get out.

Still smiling, Caleb came up on the porch. "What about me? Do I get to come in?"

"For sure," she said, before realizing how Amish that sounded. "I baked some butter cookies, probably not as good as Aenti Nancy's, but if you'd like—"

"I'd like," he said quietly.

For a minute, she couldn't look away from him. There was no amusement in his hazel eyes now, only a seriousness that set her pulse to bouncing.

It was her turn to flush. "I don't know what's wrong with me, standing here like…like…"

"Some kind of *doppick*?" he suggested, his mouth twitching.

Dummy.

"Thank you very much."

Joshua mumbled a shy greeting. As Abby led the way to the kitchen, the man and boy started talking about baseball. She knew Joshua and his friends were obsessed. He'd give a lot to see a real professional baseball game. Abby felt selfish because she'd never thought to take him to see the St. Louis Cardinals. Maybe, if she got to feeling well enough to drive…

The kitchen felt like a refuge to her. Here, she could stay busy instead of mooning over a man who was essentially a stranger. Since there was always coffee on, she was able to put mugs before both Caleb and Joshua, who drank as much of it as his *daad* and *brudder*, despite his youth. Abby put on a kettle to heat water for a cup of tea for herself, then piled cookies on a plate that she set in the middle of the table. By that time, the water was boiling, which gave her another excuse to keep her back to this caller.

Of course, once she turned with her cup of tea in hand, she found him watching her. He gestured toward the chair across from him. What could she do but sit down?

"Joshua," she said, "I never asked why you came in. Was there something you needed?"

He flushed again. "Just wanted coffee."

"I'm sure you've squeezed in a few cookies."

He grinned. "*Ja*, I will take a few for Isaac, too."

"*Sehr gutt.* Tell him to enjoy."

A sizeable pile of cookies clutched in his hand, he went out the back door.

Caleb laughed. "I wonder how many of those will make it to his brother?"

"He's always hungry."

Reaching for another cookie, he said, "I remember those days. I grew like a weed, and I could be starved ten minutes after eating dinner. Couldn't seem to fill up."

"You still seem plenty hungry." She was pretty sure he was on his third or fourth cookie, and they were huge.

"Ahh…" His hand stopped.

Abby chuckled. "As Aenti would say, eat yourself full. I'm used to it. The way Onkel Eli and the boys can sit down at the table and make heaps of food vanish in minutes still amazes me."

Caleb set the cookie on his plate. "You sound good. Are you feeling better?"

She had to think about that. "My shoulder does. My chest—" she rested a hand over her sternum "—still hurts if I bend the wrong way or move too suddenly."

His intensity was entirely focused on her. He didn't reach for his coffee, scarcely blinked. "Your head?"

She wanted to believe he cared. Trusting him even this much felt risky. What she was actually risking… She'd think about that later.

"There are times it seems to be easing, and then pain hits me out of the blue. Well, sometimes it comes out of nowhere. If I get mad or upset," she admitted, "I can count on feeling as if I'd taken an axe to my head."

"When you try to remember?"

Looking away from him, Abby still said, "Yes. It's as if I'm being punished for trying." When he didn't say anything, she lifted her gaze to his face. With sudden hostility, she said, "I suppose, like Sergeant Donahue, you don't believe I've forgotten a thing."

Lines in his forehead deepened. "I've seen instances of temporary amnesia. Your version is more extreme than most, but it's not uncommon after a blow to the head."

"Thank you for saying that, even if you don't believe it," she said stiffly.

He shocked her by reaching across the table to cover her hand with his. Looking troubled, he said, "Abby, it is my fault that Donahue knew about your appointment. I mentioned it in passing, but I wouldn't have if I'd thought he'd show up. I just wanted him to know you were doing your part to recover."

Her hand balled into a fist as she withdrew it from beneath his, too warm, too strong, too disturbing. "Nobody cares how quickly I'm recovering. You must realize I'm not welcome back to work. Even if I fought for the right to do my job, nobody trusts me."

Caleb's frown deepened. "Donahue wants to get to the bottom of what happened. You can't blame him for that. Surely the detectives you work with believe in you."

Shoving back her chair so she could push to her feet, she laughed harshly. "Sure. Didn't you hear Detective McCarthy today?"

She saw that he had.

"The sergeant is making darn sure everyone thinks I gunned Neal down. I just don't understand—" Her voice broke. She shook her head and backed away. "Take your time, I need to—"

She fled, taking with her the memory of his expression, one she didn't understand at all.

Chapter Five

Abby knelt on the mulched ground, snipping off greens and dropping them into a bucket atop the broccoli and cabbage she'd already harvested. She had to remember to pick a few tomatoes, too. Only the ripe ones, Aenti Nancy had said firmly.

Lips curving, Abby paused to look around at the tidy garden, so carefully tended. Long rows of raspberry and blackberry vines were tied to wire strung between posts. The brightly colored squash and the ripening pumpkins would feed the family and be sold at weekend farmer's markets, too. Her aunt had made Joshua fetch a watermelon from the garden earlier— she'd decreed them to be too heavy for Abby to lift and carry yet. Nor would she allow her to pick apples, or dig potatoes or sweet potatoes. Abby hadn't argued; her chest ached constantly, and she still moved her shoulder cautiously. She wouldn't want to get up on a ladder and find herself dizzy, either.

But this—being here in the garden, seeing the quickness of the blue jay taking off from a branch in an apple tree, hearing the call of a whippoorwill, was a pleasure. In the city, she forgot what she was missing.

Tomorrow, she might walk into the deep Missouri woods that backed the farm: huge old sycamores and pin oaks, dogwood and redbud. Birds, squirrels, rabbits were plentiful as, somewhere, were sleeping possums and raccoons.

Getting to her feet was still a challenge, but she'd perfected methods of rising without worsening any of her aches and pains. She always felt a tiny bit of triumph when she made it.

She bent to lift the bucket, but her eye caught a flash of light in the woods. Sun reflecting off glass or metal that shouldn't be there.

Abby's subconscious made a decision long before she could have reasoned out the wrongness of whatever that was she'd seen. She threw herself sideways, landing hard on the ground in the orchard that bordered the garden. Her sternum felt as if she'd split it in two, and lightning must have struck her head. The *crack* of a rifle being fired flooded her with remembered fear, even as she groped for a sidearm she didn't have. Operating on instinct, she tried to make herself small enough to hide behind the trunk of the closest apple tree.

Crack.

Bark peppered her face.

"Abby!" her uncle called urgently from the barn. His

booted feet thudded as he ran toward her. Then he bellowed, "You! There are people here! Quit shooting!"

He reached her, crouched above her. His hat had fallen off, she saw distantly.

"Get down!" she told him. "He might—"

"No, no. It was some fool hunting. He heard me and is hurrying home, for sure. Sorry, he'd be, if he'd shot a person, not even noticing how close he was to a farm."

The silence reassured her enough that the tension gradually drained from her muscles. Even the birds had quit calling. Abby began to breathe again. Of course Onkel Eli would think that. It would never occur to him that someone would shoot at *her*. But she didn't believe for a minute that a misguided hunter had fired from the dim cover of the woods into the sunlit garden. How could the shooter have missed seeing the house and the big barn, the clothes drying on a line, Aenti Nancy's purple dress and apron, Abby's a rich blue? No. And was it coincidence that this was the first time Abby had come out behind the house?

She groaned involuntarily when she moved to sit up. Her uncle helped her, his face creased in worry as he looked her over.

"There's blood on your face!" he exclaimed.

Abby lifted her hand. "It was the bark and bits of the tree trunk. Just scratches." Still sitting, she inspected the tree and saw a fresh groove cut by a high-powered bullet, only inches above where her head had been. "That was no accident," she said slowly. "He was shooting at *me*."

Her uncle's gaze followed hers. He didn't want to believe her, she could tell, but appalled understanding overcame his powerful faith in the goodness of his fellow man.

"God was with you," he said sturdily.

Her eyes returning to the gash in the tree trunk, she murmured, "*Ja*. He must have been."

CALEB WALKED SLOWLY into the dimness beneath the forest canopy, his pauses frequent. He scanned the earth for the glint that would give away a forgotten shell, a cigarette butt or gum wrapper or footprint. Anything to tell him where the shooter had set up— if, indeed, he hadn't been a stupid teenager swinging around to take a potshot at a bird taking flight.

He didn't like admitting that the call from Eli Kemp had shaken him. He'd driven like a crazy man, flashing lights clearing the road ahead of him even if the emergency had come and gone. Abby hadn't been hurt.

The Amish didn't call the local police for something like this, but Eli said, "If you come, then she might be willing to lie down." Either he was making a concession to his worldly niece, or he'd really been frightened.

After he arrived, Caleb had seen Abby immediately. Looking smaller than she was, she sat bent forward in a rocker in the living room. She seemed to be trying to hug herself with folded arms, holding in pain. Shocked by the change, he saw that her usually bright blue eyes were glassy and somehow darkened. Her skin stretched too tight across her cheekbones.

When he asked if she still had pain medication, she'd been slow to answer. "Yes," she said finally. "But they make me—"

"Take one," he'd snapped.

She averted her face but finally gave the tiniest of nods.

Of course she wanted to come out with him. *Cop,* he'd had to remind himself.

Now he hunted for any evidence at all of an intruder with malignant intent. The graze in the trunk of the apple tree had given him a clear direction. The shooter had to have been here, somewhere within a narrow corridor.

At last he let out a long breath, rolled his shoulders and turned back to look toward the garden and house. There was nothing. Not the smallest sign that anyone had ever stood here, far less planted a tripod or lain down to use a bipod to steady the rifle. He'd looked for any nicks in the trees here in the woods, a broken branch, and found zip.

Yes, somebody had fired a gun, there was no question. Eli and Isaac had heard it, too, as had Nancy in the house. But whether Abby had been a target Caleb couldn't confirm. Or rule out, of course, but he felt increasingly doubtful.

Abby admitted she had no idea where the first

bullet had gone. She'd heard the shot, but no thud of the bullet hitting the side of the house or anything else. The second one… It might just have been a wild shot that happened to come scarily close to Abby. If she hadn't dived for cover—and he knew he'd have done the same—the damn shot might not have come anywhere near her.

He leaned toward the stupid-teenager explanation himself, which would reassure the Kemps but make Abby mad. She'd trust him less than she already did, which he couldn't afford.

Walking back toward the house, Caleb wished he'd never agreed to try to worm his way into Abby Baker's confidence. His mixed feelings were only one of the reasons he had hated undercover work. This time…too many of those feelings were inappropriate, given the situation.

He'd long since admitted to himself that physically, she pushed his buttons. He liked his women tall, loved the length of her stride, the curves she probably cursed when she was on the job. Her contradictions drew him. The toughness that kept her chin up even when she hurt enough to have most people whimpering, the bewilderment and sense of betrayal that triggered his protective instincts big time.

If he hadn't known Mike Donahue so long, he'd probably buy into her story. He wanted to. But Donahue was right that her amnesia was damn convenient. The reason her partner was dead while she was alive didn't sit well with Caleb. Neal Walker hadn't been wearing a vest, while she was. Because she was prepared either for him to return fire or because she knew in advance that something was going down? She'd be dead, too, if not for that vest. The shoulder shot was nothing. The bang on the head had likely been accidental.

Yeah, Caleb could think of ways she might have set up the whole thing. Maybe she'd been confident no one would doubt her "sweet" face.

And maybe Donahue had his head up his butt and Abby Baker was everything she seemed to be—a strong and courageous decorated law-enforcement officer. But it was her honesty that struck him every time he saw her.

Once he passed the garden, he took the time to hunt for the bullet, too, looking for torn turf or a fresh scar in tree trunks and the wood clapboards on the house, but wasn't surprised when he didn't find any sign there, either. Bracing himself for Abby's reaction, he went in the back door.

Eli sat at the kitchen table, apparently waiting. "What did you find?"

Caleb shook his head. "Nothing."

The Amishman straightened. "A teenager, then?"

"It's possible," Caleb admitted. "I'd like to have found the bullet, but it would take an intensive search. My budget doesn't justify that when no one was injured."

"*Ja*, I understand." Eli slapped the table with his

palms and stood. "I must get back to work. Nancy is with Abby, trying to talk her into lying down."

Hearing Eli's dryness, Caleb smiled crookedly. "*Agasinish*, is she?" The Deitsch word for *stubborn, contrary*, seemed fitting.

Eli's face split in a grin that he made vanish when he heard approaching footsteps.

Nancy bustled into the kitchen. "Ach, her head hurts so!"

"Do you think she's up to talking to me before I go?" Caleb asked.

"She would fuss for sure if you didn't."

He went to the living room alone to find that Abby held ice wrapped in a thin kitchen towel to her head. Before she saw him, she sighed and moved it to her chest, which had the effect of pulling the fabric of her dress tight over her breasts.

And he knew damn well he shouldn't be noticing.

She looked up when he walked in front of her to sit on the coffee table, where his knees came close to touching hers.

"How are you?" he asked.

Predictably, she said, "Better." Her mouth crooked. "Aenti Nancy brought my pills and I took one, as ordered." She gestured to the end table, where the prescription bottle sat within reach.

"Good." A frown furrowed his brow as he met her eyes. He wanted to reassure her. Most of all, he wanted to touch her, and he couldn't. "I didn't find a thing," he made himself say. "No shells, foot-prints…nothing."

"The bullet?"

"Not that, either."

She sat very still, even her facial muscles under impressive control. Her gaze bored into his for longer than was comfortable. Then she said, "Thank you for coming," in obvious dismissal.

He scowled. "That's it? Go away?"

That stubborn chin rose. "You think like my uncle. Nobody would want to hurt *me*. It had to be some foolish teenager. Well, maybe it was, but you'll have to forgive me for not being so credulous, given that I was shot *twice* not three weeks ago. I saw the sun reflect off what had to be a gun sight. Whoever was looking through it couldn't help but see me, and he pulled the trigger anyway."

"Did you hear me disputing that? All I told you is that I can't find shells or a bullet. In fact, I'm thinking the foolish teenager wouldn't have stopped to pick up his shells." And since that was the truth, uneasiness tugged at him. "We need to let Donahue know what happened," he added.

"I feel sure you intend to do that."

Stung by the astringency in her tone even though, yeah, he was on Donahue's side, Caleb turned his head in an exaggerated show of looking for something. "Since I don't see a phone…"

"It doesn't matter." Her sudden resignation bothered him. She looked tired, any light in her eyes dimmed. "We both know what he'll think."

Conscious of an uncomfortable density in his chest, Caleb knew why. This woman was all contradictions: tough one minute, heartbreakingly vulnerable the next.

"Abby," he said, voice rough. "Give me a chance. Talk to me." For the first time, he didn't know whether this was the cop asking, or the man. "Do you believe Sergeant Donahue is out to get you?"

Obviously startled, she echoed, "Out to get me?"

"That's what I'm asking. Before the shooting, did you get the vibe he wanted you out of his unit?"

After the smallest hesitation, she said, "No. Nothing like that. He encouraged me. I thought, I don't know, that he was happy with my job performance. That's why having him turn on me without hesitation came as such a shock."

Caleb braced his elbows on his knees. "You had no doubts about your partner?"

New life—and indignation—sparked in her eyes. "Is this an interrogation?"

He hid a flinch even as he smiled. "Forgot my truncheon."

Abby made a face at him. "No, I never doubted Neal. We'd gotten to be good friends. He and his wife had me over to dinner a lot, and she talked me into trying Pilates and things I'd never done." She spread her fingers. "A mani-pedi, a lingerie party. Stuff like that."

Oh, he could picture her in lacy panties and bra no problem. And he could not afford to let her see him getting aroused. *So keep your mind on business,* he ordered himself.

"Have you talked to her since the incident? What's her name?"

Her breath hitched. "Laura. Laura Walker." Abby swallowed. "I called from the hospital. She hung up on me. Somebody must have convinced her I killed Neal."

If Donahue had, he'd been stupid. If he hadn't… maybe Neal had shared some worries about his partner with his wife.

But Caleb said only, "I'm sorry."

Lips pressed together, Abby nodded slightly. Being careful not to jar her head, he realized.

"Pain pill helping?"

"Some," she said absently, before blinking. "I mean, sure—"

"You're fine. Of course." Without knowing he was going to do it, Caleb took her hand in his. She was so fine boned, her fingers long. Oddly, given how hot it was outside, her hand felt chilly. "Your face is expressive enough to tell me when you're not fine at all."

"I do feel better," she argued. "The ice helped, too."

"Okay." Her lips were so close. All he had to do was lean forward…and her pink cheeks suggested she was thinking the same thing he was. But if he was going to live by any kind of code, he couldn't make that kind of move on her. Besides, what if he found out that she was only playing him and he'd been fool enough to fall for it? Caleb forced himself to squeeze her hand and let go, sitting up straighter to widen the distance between them. Using sexual attraction to gain her trust was a line he wouldn't cross. He said gruffly, "I wish there was something I could do to help."

"You did drive me to that appointment," she said quietly. "And you came right away today. There's nothing else."

Another dismissal…and one he had to accept.

He lingered long enough to watch her climb the staircase as if it were as imposing as Mount Everest. She clung to the handrail the whole way, resting every step or two.

Caleb ached to sweep her up into his arms and carry her to bed, where he could tenderly tuck her in. Frustrated with himself, he waited only until she'd safely reached the hall above without falling before letting himself out the front door.

IT TOOK TWO DAYS before Abby felt strong enough to walk down the long driveway and then a hundred yards or so beside the road to reach the phone shanty that was shared between four families. Of course, in the Amish way, anyone else in need was welcome to use the phone, too.

Her head kept turning. She felt unpleasantly exposed, but needed to speak to her sergeant herself. Anyway, she refused to become housebound. Maybe Onkel Eli was right, and she hadn't been the target of those two shots at all. Even if she was, surely nobody could be watching her night and day. Around here, it was true that strangers were noticed. The woods offered the best cover, and here, she was too far from them. On that thought, her gaze slid uneasily to the cornfield. She'd hid amongst the cornstalks herself as a child. A man with sniper training could ease through the rows, barely causing a ripple.

But why? She didn't remember anything. Only in her dreams did she replay the night in the alley, but the details continued to dissolve the minute she woke up, never holding their shape long enough for her to grab hold.

Once in the three-sided shanty with its slanting roof, she felt protected. No red light blinked on the answering machine today, and no neighbor had left a note saying "Abby Baker, there is a message for you."

She'd brought Sergeant Donahue's cell phone number on a slip of paper, and now she dialed it.

"Donahue," he said brusquely.

"This is Detective Baker. In case your friend the sheriff didn't already tell you, I thought you should know that two shots were fired at me Saturday."

"Doesn't sound like there's any reason to think the shooter was after you."

She stiffened. "Is that what he told you?"

Although she'd been expecting his answer, it still felt like a betrayal.

Gripping the phone tightly, she distracted herself by gazing across the gravel road to a pasture where a team of enormous chestnut-brown draft horses grazed. They could be her canary in the coal mine, she thought—she needn't be alarmed unless the horses saw something unexpected.

"He said he couldn't find any evidence either way," the sergeant said gruffly. "Just who is it you think is going after you, Baker?"

"Whoever shot Neal and me in that alley."

He snorted. "Good one. Someone just strolled up, took your weapon from you and shot your partner while you both stood paralyzed. I gotta go with the odds. Now, if you could *tell* me what happened, I might have something else to go on. But, funny thing, you can't."

"I've been a good cop." Her throat felt tight. "Honest, caring, liked by my fellow officers. I wouldn't have been promoted to detective so quickly if that wasn't true."

"Rot can hide deep, detective." His sneer could be heard. "Haven't you ever bitten into a bright red apple to find brown, wormy flesh?"

Her chest ached, and it wasn't from the cracked bone. The people she'd considered family had abandoned her, except for those who'd made the drive up here to ridicule a kind, gentle people she loved. Everything she'd worked so hard for had ceased to count. From the time her mother was killed, all she had wanted was to become a police officer, her ultimate goal always the homicide squad. She hadn't felt so lost since her father told her that her mother was dead. Gunned down in a convenience-store holdup.

Now her future had become a blank…but going back wasn't even a remote possibility.

"You know," she said, "I thought I always had someone at my back, but I was wrong. I quit. Feel free to let Personnel know. No matter what happens, I won't be back."

"If you think that makes you less of a suspect in the murder of a good man, you're wrong."

His harsh words meant nothing to her.

"Investigate all you like. You'll find nothing to implicate me." She quietly hung up the receiver, cutting off a burst of speech.

Anger and something she might call grief filled her until she wasn't sure there was room for her lungs to draw in the next breath. Even so, she had no doubt she'd done the right thing. He could come up here to interview her as he pleased, but she had no more obligation to report in, and she refused to beg anyone who should have known better to believe in her. A big slice of her memories might have been stolen from her, but Abby knew Neal would never have drawn on her, far less actually shot her…and believed as profoundly that he'd never have given her cause to have to defend herself from him.

She closed her eyes and rested her forehead on the rough plank siding of the shanty. Why couldn't she remember? *Why?*

Chapter Six

A few days after the shooting incident, Caleb stopped by the Kemp farm again. Something was immediately different this time, though. Usually when he arrived, one of the men would appear from the barn or a field, or Nancy would peek out and have the front door open long before he could reach the porch. Today, he didn't see anyone around. At first chilled at seeing the farm deserted, he suddenly realized the Kemps had probably sat down to eat their midday meal. Early, by his standards, but that was because he didn't get up at the crack of dawn.

After he knocked, it was Eli who opened the door and said, "Sheriff, come in."

"I don't want to interrupt your meal."

"No, no, you must join us. We just started."

Caleb hesitated, but chose to follow Abby's uncle. Why kid himself? To see her, he'd make a nuisance of himself. Probably already had been, come to think of it.

Silence reigned in the kitchen. Everyone appeared to be concentrating on their plates. Unless he was imagining things, tension filled the room. Had he interrupted a family argument?

The moment Nancy saw Caleb, she jumped to her feet, her determination to feed every visitor kicking in. "Joshua, get a chair for the sheriff. *Schnell, schnell!*" She shook her head at Abby, who started to rise, and set a place for him herself.

"I'm sorry," he felt compelled to say. "I didn't mean to invite myself."

He was aware that Abby glanced his way, tension on her face. Or maybe that was irritation. Because she didn't want him involved in whatever was going on?

Lucky he wasn't a sensitive guy.

"There is always plenty," Nancy assured him, but without her beaming smile.

Bowls and plates were immediately handed his way. He dished up, trying not to let greed overcome him. His midday meals tended to be light. As always when he was here, though, the temptation was great, starting with sourdough biscuits fresh from the oven.

Looking up from his full plate, he saw that Abby hadn't done more than pick at her food, while the men were already reaching for seconds.

"You talk to her!" Nancy burst out. "Abby thinks she should leave us."

"What?" Caleb had just split open a biscuit, but didn't pick up his knife to butter it. "You're nowhere near recovered."

"It's not that." She quit even pretending she was eating, setting down her fork. After one glance flicked at him, she focused on her aunt and uncle. "The last thing I wanted was to bring violence with me, to involve other people. If those shots *were* intended for me, the same person will be back. I can't even protect myself, far less my family! What if—" her voice broke "—one of you were hurt? Or Joshua, when he came in late? I couldn't live with myself."

Suspicion was his middle name. Her speech seemed melodramatic harsh, playing on the shots that may or may not have been intended for her.

"Where would you go?" her aunt asked. "Ach, someone to watch over you, you must have."

Caleb jumped in. "I agree. You can't go back to your apartment."

"I can call Dad."

The silence was so conspicuous, Caleb looked around in puzzlement. Why had she come here in the first place if her father was nearby?

It would seem they all knew something he didn't.

"You haven't mentioned your father."

Abby bent her head. "We're not close."

"You mean, he's not from the area?"

"Jefferson City."

The state capital was centrally located, and a fair distance from this corner of Missouri, but not so far from Kansas City.

"What does he do for a living?" Subtext: would the man even be around to take care of her?

"He's a researcher working on pest management for the state Department of Agriculture."

Caleb heard a muttered "Never home" he thought came from Eli.

"Married?"

She shook her head.

"Abby." He waited until she raised her eyes to meet his, her reluctance apparent. "This is a good place for you. *If* somebody is gunning for you—" he made sure she heard where he put the emphasis "—what could be safer than a rural area, where any strangers will stand out? Think about it. If that shooter was after you, where did he leave his car?" He gave her a minute, not positive why he felt an urgent need to stomp on whatever scheme she'd been trying to launch, but going with it anyway. "He'd have had a long walk, and through the woods. If he's from Kansas City, he'd have felt like he'd been plunked down in the Wild West. You think somebody can't find you in Jefferson City? There, you'd be alone all day. Here, you have family surrounding you." More quietly, he said, "You have me." Even if he didn't quite know what he meant by that.

Her lips parted as she prepared to challenge his claim, but instead their gazes locked. It was an oddly naked moment. Her eyes held turbulence, and he feared what she'd see in his. He hadn't had a chance to put up any kind of guard.

After a moment, she dipped her chin in some kind

of acquiescence and went back to poking at the food on her plate. Caleb decided to eat while he could.

He and Eli discussed the weather, a perennial topic in farming country, and particularly when forecasters were expressing concern that conditions might be leading to tornadoes. Caleb's attention was only half on what was said, while half remained on Abby, who stood the moment Nancy did to begin clearing the table.

Studying her, he realized the strain on her face when he first walked in might have to do with her purported fear for her family, but also with the headache that wouldn't release its grip on her.

When he thought she'd done enough to help Nancy, he said, "Abby, can we talk for a minute?"

Caleb didn't like seeing her wariness toward him, even if he deserved it.

"Yes," she said after a moment, drying her hands and hanging up a dish towel. "But I only have a few minutes. Joshua is to drive me into town—"

"For your physical-therapy appointment. That's why I stopped by." A small piece of why. "I'll be happy to drive you and save Joshua the trip."

"That's very kind of you," she said stiffly. "Onkel Eli, you heard that?"

"Ja," he agreed. "It is a kindness, and I have work for Joshua."

The kid, obviously crushed but resigned, clapped his hat on his head and went out the back door.

"Why don't we leave now, and I'll buy you an ice-cream cone before your appointment?" he suggested. He wasn't sure he could eat another bite, but given the little food she'd put away, ice cream might be perfect.

She perked up. "At Miller's?"

The general store sold half a dozen flavors of hard ice cream made by an Amish dairy farmer from a freezer behind the counter. Their idea of a scoop was the size of a softball.

He smiled. "Where else?"

CALEB'S SMILES, WHETHER AMUSED, sexy or unnervingly tender, invariably weakened Abby's defenses.

"That sounds good," she admitted. "Thank you."

Within minutes, she was in Caleb's SUV, waiting for the air conditioner to kick in. Fortunately, the wait wasn't long. They were still on the gravel road when she felt the first cool air.

"Let me know if that gets too cold," he said.

The heat and humidity today had sapped Abby's energy and appetite both.

"Are you kidding?" She basked in the chill. "I helped can green beans this morning, and it was *roasting* in the kitchen, even with the doors and windows open. How women did it when stoves were wood burning I can't imagine." She made a face. "I've been spoiled rotten. Air-conditioning in my apartment, my car, the police station…"

The corner of his mouth curled. "Your department vehicle. Grocery stores, banks…" The glance he flicked at her no longer held amusement. "Your head hurts."

"I'm not doing so well hiding it, huh?"

"No. Damn it, Abby. I think you need to see a doctor again."

"It hasn't been that long."

"Memories?"

She'd give a lot to be able to trust him.

Understanding her silence deepened the lines in his forehead. Was he insulted? After a minute, he said quietly, "Would you believe me if I promise not to share anything you've remembered with Donahue?"

"Are you promising?" Abby did believe him, which might be foolish. But it wasn't as if she knew anything meaningful.

"Yeah." He took his right hand from the steering wheel and captured her hand with it.

Electricity ran up her arm.

"Okay." The word sounded scratchy. "I'm having flashes. Some from the days before the shooting. Totally unrelated stuff. Some trivial, like thinking about looking for a new apartment. I won't need to be near the precinct."

"Why not?"

"Sergeant Donahue didn't tell you? I quit."

He nodded. No questions. She saw a muscle flex in his jaw and wondered what that was about.

Abby reverted to the disturbing subject of the fleeting memories that had taken to blindsiding her. "I had this really vivid picture of myself standing in this line at the grocery store, people getting grumpy around me because an old lady was so slow paying. She had a little trouble with figuring out which end of her card to insert, but mostly she just wanted to linger and have someone to talk to. The clerk was being really nice. I wanted to slap the guy in line in front of me and say, *Why don't you tease her? Talk to her nicely, instead of asking if she can't get it right? Offer to carry her grocery bag out for her as soon as your stuff is rung up? Make her day?*" Seeing Caleb's crooked smile, she felt her cheeks heat. "Okay, I have a little Amish in me."

"More than a little, I think." The warmth in his slow, deep voice was reassuring.

"And then…" Her headache intensified, letting her know she was edging into dangerous territory. She kept going nonetheless. "I remember begging Neal to tell me what had him so alarmed. Even scared. It's just this flash, the two of us sitting in our car at the curb, me sure something was really wrong. I already knew he was worried, but this was different. It was as if…" A stab of pain felt like an ice pick. She squeezed her eyes shut.

"Abby?" The SUV swerved and then Caleb braked and brought it to a stop.

On the shoulder of the road, she saw, squinting.

When had the sun become so glaring she couldn't bear it?

The next moment, he wrapped his hand around her nape beneath the *kapp* and began to knead, his fingers digging into muscles and too-tight tendons. She stifled a moan.

The SUV rocked slightly and she realized a semi had sped past them. They must be on the shoulder beside the highway.

"Tell me you're okay." He sounded worried. Even scared.

Scared. "I think Neal was scared," she whispered. "Not the for-his-life kind, but as if whatever he thought he knew was huge."

The hand on her neck briefly went still. When the massage resumed, Caleb said dryly, "Terrorist-bomb scared? Mayor-of-the-city-corrupt scared? Or wife-cheating-on-him scared?"

Abby took a deep breath and straightened in her seat, sorry to lose the feel of Caleb's hand on her bare skin. "Not his wife. That's more freaked than scared." Although, what did she know? "And… I'm pretty sure this had to do with our jobs. Even before the period I can't remember, he'd take me along when he went to talk to people. He was investigating *something.* I'd hang back, just there in case he needed me, you know?"

"What kind of people?" His voice sharp, he was suddenly all cop.

"All different. Bartenders, once a biker. Pimps. Oh, and a man who looked like a mob boss. I mean, suit and tie, and he had a semicircle of beefy guys around him, all of whom were carrying. That time we were in front of a warehouse by the river. Nobody else around. It was really creepy. I kind of hovered where I could see Neal, even knowing there wasn't a thing I could do in time if he ticked the guy off."

Caleb swore. "Or to protect yourself. Damn it, he shouldn't have taken you."

"We're partners." She bit her lip. "Were partners." She hadn't quite accepted that Neal really was dead. She didn't remember seeing him go down, if she had, and she hadn't been able to attend the funeral.

Caleb's grunt sounded unhappy. "Partners are honest with each other."

"I think he was trying to protect me." That answer came from her heart. She had no proof. "He was stepping into something that could have gotten him in big trouble, and he wanted to keep me out of it in case he was wrong."

"And yet you were with him. Who'd have believed you didn't know? Whether he meant to or not, he put you at risk."

Abby looked down at her hands, clasped on her lap. Caleb was right, of course, because she had no doubt that whatever Neal had been looking into was the reason he'd been murdered, and she'd been shot. If not for a passerby…

"Did you tell Donahue any of this?"

"Of course I did!" she said indignantly. "He obviously thought I'd made it all up."

A grunt was Caleb's sole response, although she could tell as he got back on the road and drove that he was mulling over what she'd told him. Increasingly, Abby knew if there were to be answers, she'd have to find them herself. Which would mean either moving back to her apartment or collecting her car and some of her working wardrobe so that she could pass unremarked during trips to the city. She was pretty sure she could find some of the places she and Neal had gone. Unfortunately, she could no longer show a badge to compel cooperation. At least, not legitimately.

She'd love to think Caleb could be an ally, but his past friendship with Donahue meant his loyalties were already claimed. How could she even ask?

If there was some way to be sure he hadn't passed what she'd told him on to Donahue, maybe she could trust him that much.

Yes, but how would she ever know?

"Miller's," he said, and she blinked. They'd arrived.

"No, THERE'S BEEN no second attempt on her life, if that's what it was. Don't you trust me?" Irritated, Caleb kept the phone to his ear as he peered into his freezer. A casserole dish labeled Chicken Curry and Rice caught his eye. Tuning out Donahue's rumblings, he grabbed it, studied the sticky note on top with directions for heating and popped it in the microwave. He was grateful to the young Amishwoman who cleaned for him and cooked and froze several meals a week, all while he was on duty. He left her money; she left grocery lists for him.

Caleb replayed what Mike had been saying about expecting results by now: was he too busy setting up speed traps to fund his department, or had he fallen for a pretty face and a flimsy story?

He interrupted. "Why didn't you tell me she'd quit the job?"

"Ah, you know she doesn't mean it. Truth is, I'd be happy to have her back if we can clear her."

Caleb gave an incredulous laugh. "You actually think she'd work for you again?"

"She told me in the interview that Homicide had always been her goal. Somebody she loved was murdered."

Leaning a hip against the counter, Caleb frowned. "Who?"

"Didn't say."

Friend? Sibling? Or the mother who'd left the Amish faith?

"She hasn't admitted to recovering any memories?" Donahue asked. "Real or fake?"

"You set me back by days when you got in her face in front of the clinic," Caleb said. He'd try to avoid straight-out lying. "I'd gotten her talking to me, and then *kaboom*. But I've got to be honest. I don't think she's faking the memory loss, and I don't see her as a killer. If you're not already doing it, you should spread your net."

"She has gotten to you." His onetime partner's disgust came through.

"No." Yes. Hell. "I'm good at judging people, Mike. You know that."

"That's it?" Donahue sounded surly, reminding Caleb that he'd never liked any suggestion he was wrong. "Do you have a speck of evidence to support the conclusion that she's innocent?"

"Ever heard of the concept *Innocent until proven guilty*?"

"I just want to *know*." Frustration boiled in his voice.

Caleb sympathized. He'd feel the same if one of his young deputies had been gunned down. So he said, "I'm still on it. I'll do my best to get that proof, one way or another."

The two men let it go at that. Sitting down to eat twenty minutes later, Caleb was still brooding. He either should have bowed out—or he should have stamped out every spark of attraction and sympathy he felt. Liking, too. As it was, he hated lying to Abby. And now he was lying to Donahue as well.

He'd hardly made a dent in the chicken curry when he caught himself staring into space while his dinner went cold. No, he realized, backing out on his agreement with Mike Donahue wouldn't happen… because *he* had to know, too. He couldn't so much as touch Abby Baker the way he wanted to until he'd ruled out any possibility that something he couldn't even imagine had driven her to set up that damn scene in the alley.

Maybe it was time he did some quiet investigating of his own.

ABBY SAT IN the shade of the front porch, her feet bare and her sleeves rolled up. Temperatures hadn't relented, even in the waning days of September. Today was particularly hot and sticky, and she'd give a lot to be able to change into shorts and a tank top. At least her feet were bare. There wasn't anything close to a breeze, but she kept hoping for one anyway, wriggling her toes like a child reveling in the freedom of summer. Not that she didn't have a chore to do: Aenti Nancy had her shucking corn. *Lots* of corn. As fast as she worked, Nancy replaced the pile, taking the ears into the house. There, she sliced the kernels off the cobs and bagged them to freeze enough to see them through the year. Most of the crop would be sold; already this morning, Isaac had delivered a wagon full to the produce auction house on the outskirts of town.

Rip. Tearing at the husks had been satisfying

when Abby started, but her hands were getting tired. Picking out the corn silk was finicky.

When she heard a car engine, her head came up. A first spurt of excitement dismayed her, as did the pang of disappointment when she realized she didn't know the engine sound. A produce buyer to see Onkel Eli, perhaps?

But the older blue pickup truck stopped closest to the house, right where Caleb always parked. Of all people, Sam Kirk got out and walked across the lawn to the porch.

Surveying her, he grinned. "You look like you're about ten years old. Ah…" His gaze lowered, then shied from her. "Maybe not that."

Because her figure was definitely not a child's. She made a face at him. "I was just thinking the same. Remember what it felt like when the bell rang at the end of the last day of school?"

He laughed. "Free at last."

Sam Kirk. Who'd think it? And… Sam Kirk in worn chinos, athletic shoes with grass stains and a plain T-shirt?

"I didn't expect to see you," she added, carefully.

He shoved his hands in his pockets, something about his stance making her think he felt awkward. "You've been on my mind since I drove you up here. You looked pretty puny, you know." He shrugged. "I thought you might need someone to talk to."

She'd be touched if she could believe he was genuine. He *looked* sincere, but this might be a well-perfected technique when he was interviewing witnesses and suspects. How could she know?

"I already have a designated cop, ready and willing to hear my deepest secrets," she said dryly.

Sam raised his eyebrows. "Who?"

"The local sheriff. Apparently, he was KCPD for years and worked with Sergeant Donahue along the way."

"Really? I didn't hear about him."

And was perturbed because he hadn't, if she was reading his expression right. And who could blame him? He was supposed to be Donahue's partner on this investigation.

"Why don't you come up here and sit down?" To an Amish man or woman, all visitors were welcome and treated well. Nature or nurture, she felt the same compulsion—except when those visitors insulted her family. Sam had been an exception in that respect. "Would you like a cup of coffee?"

He sat on an Adirondack chair near her seat on a bench. "Not if it's any trouble. I drink more of it than I should."

Predictably, Aenti Nancy popped out. Within minutes, she brought coffee and a plate holding several chocolate whoopie pies with cream-and-vanilla filling. Sam thanked her and took a big bite.

After he finished the first of what was essentially

a huge cookie and sipped coffee, he sighed. "I may start visiting regularly."

"You and the sheriff. He's here so much, he's probably had to let out his belt a notch or two by now." At least she sounded humorous instead of cranky.

He smiled. After putting away two of the whoopie pies, Sam groaned and set the plate with the two remaining on the floorboards to one side of his chair. She couldn't help noticing he'd taken only a couple of sips of coffee. In the city, he'd be drinking it iced.

"I hear you resigned," he said.

She grabbed another ear of corn. "In my circumstances, wouldn't you have?" *Rip.*

"Probably." He hesitated. "Do you have any questions about the investigation?"

She did, but how honest would he be?

"Please tell me the witness who saw someone bending over me is being taken seriously."

"I'm confident he saw someone."

"Of course, it might have been some lowlife intending to steal my gun."

"That's…a possibility."

Okay, however reluctant, Sam *had* been honest.

She asked more questions, he answered. Unfortunately, it became apparent that the investigation was going nowhere. They were waiting for her to remember what she'd seen…or were trying to nail down proof that would justify her arrest.

Sam had just asked if she'd remembered anything

at all when Abby heard a new arrival. Not answering, she turned her head to see a black sheriff's-department vehicle pull up behind Sam's old pickup.

"Sheriff Tanner," she said simply.

She glanced back at Sam to see an intense flash of anger as he watched Caleb slam his door and start across the grass toward them.

Since they were presumably on the same side— what was *that* about?

Chapter Seven

Caleb didn't once take his eyes from the man sitting so comfortably on the Kemp porch, body language and expression implying he and Abby were best friends. Average height, dark hair, olive complexion, he looked vaguely familiar. Someone from KCPD. Given that she'd been running off her fellow detectives, why the chummy atmosphere with this one?

About the time he reached the foot of the porch steps, she smiled at him, if a bit wryly. "Caleb. Do you know Detective Sam Kirk? Sam, this is Sheriff Caleb Tanner."

Kirk set his coffee cup on the wide arm of the chair and rose to his feet. "Tanner. Abby was just telling me about you."

"All good, I hope," he said easily.

"I explained that you're my designated cop and confidant," she said, tart if you were listening for it, "and that he could have saved himself the trip."

"She's not buying that I came as a friend," Sam said ruefully.

Caleb shot back. "Possibly because you're one of the lead investigators into what happened to her."

Sam opened his mouth, but at the same moment Nancy pushed open the screen door. "Sheriff! So lucky Abby is, to have two visitors today! I'll bring you coffee."

"Denke," he said, offering her an affectionate smile.

Sam bent and picked up the plate, holding it out. "Plenty of leftovers."

Nancy tut-tutted, snatched the plate and hurried back into the house. Amused, Caleb could read her mind. *Leftovers! Those were for family, not a valued visitor.* Assuming that's how she saw him.

Unfortunately, the tableau remained: Abby holding a half-shucked cob in her hands, Sam rocking back on his heels, his hands in his pockets, smiling, and Caleb feeling like a third wheel. Aggressive, too. He didn't like another man laying a subtle claim to his girl. Yeah, he felt that primitive. He wouldn't be leaving until Kirk did—unless something exceptionally bad occurred in his county, demanding his presence. He willed the radio to stay silent.

Caleb strolled across the porch and sat on the same bench as Abby, leaning back against the house wall and stretching out his legs. *Yep, I'm at home here. Suck eggs.*

In another mood, he'd have laughed at himself.

"So, what's your perspective on the investigation?" he asked.

Kirk talked in circles, which wasn't a surprise. How up-front was he likely to be in front of a suspect? What Caleb couldn't tell was whether the detective agreed with his sergeant or not.

Nancy brought out coffee and a plate of whoopie pies for Caleb. When she offered to refill Sam Kirk's cup, he must have recognized his cue to go.

His voice became gentle when he said his good-byes to Abby. "I meant my offer—any time you want to take me up on it. I think you've gotten a rough deal, and I don't like it."

She stood and thanked him. They didn't touch. He gave her a nod and strode back to his pickup truck. After doing a U-turn, he waved as he passed the house.

Silence enveloped the two left on the porch.

"Your hands look sore," Caleb said at last, nodding at them.

Abby scrunched up her nose. "I'm not used to doing manual labor, but I'm determined to keep up with Aenti Nancy."

He laughed. "I don't blame you. How about if I help you for a few minutes?"

"Do you mean that?" She plucked at her dress, trying to let air in.

His gaze dropped to her hand, making her realize she'd pulled the fabric over her breasts. When their eyes met, she felt even hotter.

He cleared his throat. "Sure, unless I get called away." He went inside to wash his hands, then returned to join her in shucking corn.

He'd been at it for a few minutes when she said, "You really don't have to do this."

He smiled. "I came out to see you. I can make myself useful at the same time."

"What would the county council members think if they knew they were paying you to do this?"

Caleb grinned at her. "We'll call it my lunch hour." After a minute, he asked, "Why was *he* here?"

Giving him a sharp look, she said, "Do we have a little jurisdictional conflict here?"

"It was just a question." And the conflict didn't have a thing to do with their respective jurisdictions; it was all about her.

Tiny creases formed in her forehead. "The answer is *I don't know*. He's claimed before that he thinks Sergeant Donahue is wrong to suspect me. Today he offered to answer questions and listen if I wanted to talk."

Caleb heard the undertone. After dropping corn husks atop the pile in the nearly full bin, he said, "You don't believe him."

Abby shrugged. "Hard to."

"And that goes double for me?"

She gave him a wary, sidelong look. "I...don't know. I haven't decided about you yet."

"Huh. I'm encouraged."

The corners of her lips quivered. He loved her

mouth, whether it was pursed or smiling or she was nibbling on her lower lip.

Can't touch her.

Conversation strayed as they worked. She told him Joshua yearned from afar for a younger Amish girl. "Too young, thank goodness," Abby said. "Both of them, in my opinion. But she's very pretty. I looked for her Sunday."

He nodded; this had been the church Sunday for all three of the local Amish districts. On alternate Sundays, each district worshipped at the home of one of the members. The following Sunday was for visiting.

"Poor Joshua is not alone in having his eye on her." Abby shook her head, the ribbons dangling from her *kapp* moving over the swell of her generous breasts beneath her blue dress. "I thought she seemed a tiny bit self-satisfied and vain, but I may be wrong."

Caleb laughed. In Deitsch, he said, "Ach, but weren't you the prettiest girl at that age?"

Her smile faded. "I was mostly living with my father then."

"Mostly?"

"I still came summers, and sometimes spring or Christmas breaks."

After the lighter, enjoyable conversation, perhaps he shouldn't ask, but curiosity overcame Caleb. He tried to keep his voice soft, undemanding. "Will you tell me why?"

"My father didn't remarry, and I guess having me home alone every day didn't strike him as a good idea."

"And earlier?"

Her hands had gone still. "He…didn't deal well with my mother's death. He didn't have anything left for me."

The man had a young daughter grieving as much as he was, and he couldn't be bothered with her? It was all Caleb could do to hold back what he really thought.

"You haven't said—"

His radio crackled. "Sheriff?"

A minute later, he was on his feet. "I have to go."

Obviously worried, Abby stood, too, a hand pressed to her chest. "I didn't hear all of that. Did she say a buggy…?"

"Yes." A deputy old enough to know better had gotten so excited about nailing a speeder, he hadn't given a thought to the vulnerability of a portion of their citizenry. Grimly, Caleb said, "I forbid high-speed chases in this county for a good reason. The driver of the car my deputy was after took off when he saw that he was being pursued. Raced over a rise and hit a buggy." He shook his head at her expression. "I know two people were transported to the hospital, but not how badly they're hurt, or who they are."

"Oh, no." Worry—*caring*—were plain to see in her blue eyes. "Can you tell me where it happened?"

"Jenner Road. It probably wasn't anyone in your aunt and uncle's district…"

"But you can't be sure." She reached out as if she couldn't help herself and squeezed his hand. "Can you let us know? That is, if we don't hear in the meantime?"

Despite his tension, he smiled. "Because the Amish grapevine works faster than police radio. I will, Abby."

The impulse to kiss her was so visceral, he felt as if he never parted from her without at least a quick kiss. Fighting the odd feeling, he reluctantly released her hand and then made himself bound down the porch steps and lope across the lawn.

TENSION GRIPPED THE entire household. Abby's uncle had allowed Joshua to stay at the house to help his aunt.

The injured Amish would be acquaintances of the Kemps, at least. Very possibly members of their church district, friends, even first or second or third cousins of Abby's. The Amish men and women in the county all knew each other, if only through business. The injured might be the butcher and his wife, the very fine quilter who owned the fabric store in town, the young couple who only Sunday had shyly let friends know they were expecting their first child. Or Rose and her husband… Surely not them.

Neighbors and friends had heard there was an accident and assumed the Kemps, who had become so friendly with the sheriff, must know more. Visitors came and went. Aenti sent Joshua to the phone shanty twice to check for messages.

Aenti Nancy wouldn't be alone in setting to cooking. The Amish women always saw to it that nobody who was injured or mourning would need to prepare a meal for weeks to come. Levi Graber, the buggy maker, let it be known that he would repair or replace the damaged buggy without recompense. The loss of a buggy horse, many of which were retired harness racers, would be a great loss, all agreed. Everyone prayed that no children had been hurt.

Abby had almost forgotten how intertwined were the lives of the Amish spread across the county, and beyond. How they could truly count on each other. The Leit, as they called themselves—the people— didn't believe in insurance or the government Social Security. Medical bills would be settled by the entire church district, unless they were too great, in which case other groups would contribute as well. Bake sales might be held, or a quilt auction, or farming equipment they could do without might be sold, just as they did to support the local volunteer firefighters, many of whom were Amish.

They all prayed for the driver of the car, too, that he not be badly hurt. They felt sure he was sorry for his mistake; the injured people in the buggy would forgive him, and so should everyone else.

This represented a painful contrast with what Abby had become accustomed to seeing on the job. Drug addiction, alcoholism, poverty and greed brought such tragedy, damaged these very connections.

Three hours later, a buggy rolled up to the barn. Hurrying out, Abby recognized Mary and Lloyd Stoltzfus. Mary was Nancy's sister, Lloyd a farrier. Before they had their feet on the ground, word had already spread.

Hurt, *ja*, but no one killed. The two in the buggy had been Ernest Wagler and his oldest son, Paul, who belonged to a neighboring church district. The worries were not over. Their bishop was with them, Paul had a broken leg that would keep him from working for a month or two, and Ernest had hit his head and was still unconscious two hours ago, when Mary and Lloyd had been at the hospital to see Lloyd's *daad*, who was in for a heart procedure.

Pain spiked in Abby's head. She knew what Ernest Wagler would experience when—if—he opened his eyes to find himself in such a strange place, with a head that felt like a grenade after someone pulled out the pin. Would he remember everything up to the moment when the buggy splintered into the ditch, or would his brain, like hers, choose to black out some of that time?

"We saw Sheriff Tanner," Mary told a cluster of women. "He asked if we could stop by here so that the Kemps would know what happened. To keep a promise, he said."

Hovering at the back of the group, Abby told herself there wasn't a reason in the world why she should be disappointed instead of pleased that he had done what he'd said he would.

No—she wasn't good at lying to herself, even when the truth was unpalatable. *My father hardly remembers he* has *a daughter.* That was a truth she had faced a very long time ago.

This truth was different: she'd wanted to see Caleb again. Her heart lifted every time she saw him. She almost trusted him. Worst of all—she felt too much for him, trust and attraction only the beginning.

For the first time in her life, she had met a man she thought she could love. *If* it didn't turn out that she'd deluded herself about who he really was—an entirely realistic possibility.

After hearing everything Mary and Lloyd had to say, Abby returned to the kitchen to share the news and to help her aunt as much as she could. Two more of Eli and Nancy's children, with their spouses and young kids, joined them for dinner that night, crowding the kitchen.

Head throbbing by the time the guests had left, Abby helped put the finishing touches on the kitchen. With the family gathered, Onkel Eli settled in the living room to read passages from the Bible, as he did every night. Abby murmured an apology and slipped outside instead.

Not even seven o'clock and it was already dark. She hadn't paid attention to the passing weeks, but the first of October had to be almost upon them. She'd never expected to stay this long. Vaguely, she'd supposed she would be cleared and back to work by now.

Her cracked sternum still twinged with incautious movements but wouldn't have kept her from studying crime scenes, conducting interviews or spending hours on end on the phone—usually on hold. But even if she had been exonerated, the ever-present headache that worsened without warning would have kept her on leave. Then, of course, there was her lost memory. No matter whether evidence turned up that led Sergeant Donahue and Sam Kirk to make an arrest, how could she do a job when everyone around her, and maybe herself most of all, would doubt the accuracy of all her memories? What if newer ones were slipping into whatever fissure had swallowed the lost week, or jumbling with old ones? Defense attorneys would call open season on her whenever she testified in a courtroom.

Abby chose to sit on the bench where she'd spent a good part of the day shucking corn, partly because it was out of the rectangle of light from the living room. The temperature probably hadn't dropped much yet, but compared to the sweltering kitchen, the air felt cool to her. She closed her eyes and drank in the quiet sounds of the evening.

How can I do the job?

She pulled herself up short. Wrong verb tense. How could she *have* done it was more to the point.

She'd already resigned. Or was that a little bit of memory slippage?

No, she couldn't return to work with those same people. She just hadn't let herself think about the future yet, beyond striving to remember what terrible things she'd seen in that alley. Clearing her name.

If she couldn't do that… No, she wouldn't believe that was even a possibility.

But once it happened…would she look for a job in another department? Or consider a different future?

Since absolutely nothing came to mind, she had to accept that she still wasn't ready to think ahead, far less make decisions.

That was the moment she first heard the growl of an approaching vehicle.

CALEB DIDN'T KNOW what he was doing here. He had no doubt that Mary and Lloyd Stoltzfus would have stopped by hours ago—and probably at nearly every other Amish household they'd passed on their way home. At this time of night, he'd be intruding. And yet he parked by the house. He couldn't believe he hungered like this to see one face.

With a sigh, he got out and started toward the front door. He'd keep it brief, say he'd just wanted to be sure they knew about the Waglers.

Something moved in the darkness on the porch, and somehow he knew.

He stopped halfway up the steps. "Abby?"

"Caleb." She sounded both puzzled and glad. The glad part made him feel a little less foolish.

As he crossed the porch to join her, he caught a glimpse through the lighted window of Nancy sitting in a recliner knitting, her head bent over her work. "Are you okay?" he asked.

"Oh…mostly tired. Once we were done freezing a whole lot of corn, we cooked for the Waglers. And people kept stopping by, of course." She added in a rush, "Thank you for making sure we knew what happened."

Mostly tired? That meant her head still ached.

"I didn't know if you'd get a phone message."

"We would have today. Joshua checked the answering machine a couple of times."

Enough soft light came from a window behind him to allow him to see her face. In her old-fashioned garb, wearing the filmy white prayer *kapp*, she made him think of a Renaissance painting, golden light against the dark. Sitting beside her, he reached for her hand and was relieved when she returned the clasp.

"Has he regained consciousness?" she asked. "Ernest?"

Caleb let out a long breath. He wished he could give her a different answer. "No. His wife says he has a hard head and will be fine, although I suspect she's mostly trying to convince herself. Doctors do seem to be optimistic, though. They think it's the swelling around his brain."

"Oh." Her face showed only in profile. "That's

what they said about me, too. They drilled a hole in my skull to relieve the swelling. Did you know that?"

His hand tightened on hers. "No."

"I wonder if he'll remember the accident."

"He may not. I told you I've seen other cases like yours."

"I wasn't sure if I believed you."

"It's the truth."

"Then why—" She stopped.

Not even breathing, he waited.

"Why doesn't anybody believe me?"

"You mean why doesn't *Donahue* believe you." Anger roughened his voice.

Abby looked fully at him. "Do you? Really?"

"Yeah." In that instant, he hadn't the smallest doubt. Not about this.

She nodded, just a dip of her head, and looked away again.

After a minute, he broke the quiet between them. "I'm surprised Eli hasn't come out to see who is here."

"I think he must have guessed."

"I'm not offending his sense of what's proper?"

"He might get confused sometimes, but mostly he knows I'm Englisch, a police officer, no *maidal* like his daughters were, that I don't need protecting."

Caleb knew better than to say so, but he wasn't so sure about that. Her strength showed, but he also often sensed vulnerability that he wouldn't expect in a woman who'd made a success of herself in law enforcement. Coming from a background like hers, she must walk an emotional maze every day.

He wanted to ask why there wasn't a man in her life, but he couldn't do that, either, not yet. Today, he hadn't been able to help wondering about Sam Kirk, though.

"Are you and Kirk friends?" he asked gruffly.

"Sam?" she said in surprise. "No, I've never even worked with him before. Although, after I was released from the hospital, he's the one who drove me here. I assumed he was playing good cop to the sergeant's bad. Thinking he could persuade me to open up to him."

"Have you?"

She laughed softly, with a hint of sadness. "No. He may really sympathize with me, I can't be sure, but…it seems unlikely."

Would Donahue have been stupid enough to overkill in sending two different cops to worm their way into her confidence? Caleb speculated. Maybe Sam Kirk did disagree with his sergeant's conclusions. Or maybe—

"Is he married?"

"Sam? I think I heard that he's divorced. Something about how much he hates to work days when he's supposed to have his kids." Abby seemed to mull that over. "You think…? No, it can't be that," she said after a minute. "He'd have asked me out before."

There were reasons he might not have. He was

quite a bit older than Abby, and relationships between cops who worked together were discouraged, if not entirely forbidden. The guy may have seen his chance when Abby needed help—and when the possibility was good that she wouldn't be back at KCPD.

Caleb kept quiet.

"It doesn't really matter," she said. "How often is he likely to show up this far from home?"

Caleb knew he ought to leave. He'd indulged himself longer than he should have. He'd be happy to sit here for hours, as long as he was holding Abby's hand.

Sure. Wouldn't want another thing, would you?

He rubbed his free hand over his jaw, feeling the scratch of evening stubble. "I should get going."

"Oh!" Abby snatched her hand back and leapt to her feet. "You must be dying to get home, and I've kept you."

"No." He rose, too, slowly. Somehow, words he hadn't meant to say came out. "I wanted to see you."

This *oh* came out differently. They faced each other, not quite touching, but near enough he could lift a hand to her cheek. In fact, he was doing it without any conscious decision.

Alarm bells went off. He had to use the brains God gave him. *Back away*, he ordered himself. *Say good-night.*

He did neither. Instead, he cupped her face and

bent forward, giving her time to retreat. To his profound relief, she swayed toward him, whispered, "Caleb?"

His lips covered hers.

Chapter Eight

His brief hesitation told Abby he was giving her a chance to slip away. She ought to take it, instead of demonstrating how inept she was at this and thus humiliating herself. What's more, this man could really hurt her. Was almost guaranteed to hurt her.

He was also the only man who'd ever inspired an unfamiliar need to touch him, to press her body against his, to crawl inside his skin if she could.

Maybe there wasn't really a choice at all. She heard herself whisper his name and laid a hand on his chest.

His lips brushed softly over hers, then more firmly when they came back for more. Rapt, she soaked in every tiny sensation. His hard chest rose and fell beneath her splayed hand. At a damp stroke along the seam of her lips, she jerked, the effect like an electrical shock. His tongue…he wanted in. Abby parted her lips and felt the hot slide of his tongue against hers.

From that moment, her thoughts blurred. A moan

slipped out. The kiss deepened, became hungry—
teeth and lips and tongue. He gathered her in with
both arms, and she pushed herself up on tiptoe to
meet him. With one hand he kneaded her butt, lift-
ing her, pulling her tighter against his tall, powerful
body, into the rigid evidence of his arousal that she
ached to feel between her thighs. Her own fingers
slid into his hair, thick and cool. She felt shameless,
urgent, all longing and need.

He was the one to groan and wrench his mouth
away. At first he kissed his way across her cheek,
sucked on her ear lobe, nipped her neck. But instead
of coming back for more, his arms loosened. She
sank back onto her heels, a chill moving through her.

Gripping her upper arms, he stepped back. His
eyes were so dark, she couldn't see any color, and
yet they glittered. His mouth was softer than she remembered seeing it, swollen. She reached up to touch
her own cheek where it burned. From the scrape
of his beard stubble, Abby realized in some distant
part of her.

"I guess that was good-night." She sounded ap-
propriately sardonic, when she felt like…like a snow
globe, just shaken. So much floating inside, no way
of knowing how the landscape would look when it
all settled.

"Your uncle could come out anytime," Caleb said
hoarsely.

She searched his face to see why he pulled back.

She only nodded, backed away herself and crossed her arms, trying desperately to hold herself together.

"It's all right, Caleb. Stick your head in and say hello if you want."

"I can't." He sounded rueful, and she knew why he couldn't let anyone else see him.

Her nod was meaningless.

"I'll be sure you get an update on Ernest."

"Thank you." *Go*, she thought fiercely. *Please go.*

"Damn it, Abby—" Intense frustration infused his voice, but then he shook his own head. "I do need to leave."

Still he kept looking at her. She wasn't sure she so much as took a breath. At last, at last, he backed up a step, then another. Finally, without another word, he departed.

She stood there, unmoving, until the SUV had disappeared down the driveway, until she could no longer hear it. Then she sank onto the bench and bent over, dizzy, her head pounding with each beat of her heart.

She didn't know if she was hurt…or aching for something that wouldn't happen.

WHAT IN *HELL* had he been thinking? Caleb asked himself violently. But he knew—he hadn't been thinking at all. All he'd been able to think about was kissing the woman since the first time he'd laid eyes on her, and tonight, the two of them alone in the warm night, there'd been a compelling sense of intimacy that undermined his resolve.

He clenched his teeth. With her looks, she'd be a natural at playing men, making them see something that didn't go deeper than the surface. God help him; he didn't believe that, but he needed to follow through on the promise he'd made to Mike Donahue.

What he wanted to do was step right smack in the middle of the investigation. Get out there himself, talk to anyone her partner had tracked down, guy with the bodyguards included. Pimps, she'd said. That struck a wrong note, assuming drugs had anything to do with the shooting in the alley. Had Donahue had the sole witness sit down with a police artist? The best of them could pull amazing details from people who thought they hadn't seen anything. Damn it; Caleb wanted to sit down with that witness himself.

Of course, he'd seriously alienate Donahue if he did any of that. Chasing leads on a crime that had happened in another part of the state did not fall in his job description.

His headlights picked out an animal in the middle of the road ahead. Braking, he watched as the possum finally scuttled into the undergrowth.

According to Donahue, Abby had left both her laptop and her phone behind. They'd gotten into her laptop, found nothing work related except notes and drafts of reports that corresponded with assigned investigations. They hadn't been able to break the password for her phone. Caleb presumed she had guessed her apartment would be searched, including the electronic devices she'd left behind.

Which left a logical next step for him, under-handed though it was.

Well, then, don't get caught, he told himself.

HE WAS TOO tied up the next couple of days to make it back out to the Kemp farm. His deputies raided a meth lab hidden in a ramshackle barn and, after a scuffle, made three arrests. Two of the three weren't even twenty-one, and this would already be their second convictions for manufacturing meth. The third guy was a scrawny sixteen-year-old who'd be tried in juvenile court.

All three yelled *police brutality*, although the only person injured in the melee was one of the deputies, who had suffered a broken cheekbone, a giant lump on his head and a heck of a shiner. After taking a two-by-four to the head, he was lucky not to have ended up in a coma like Ernest Wagler had. The good news was that Ernest's wife was right about how hard his head was; he'd regained consciousness yesterday.

The punks who'd been cooking up meth would be facing charges of assaulting a law-enforcement of-ficer as well as the drug charges. The surprise was that they hadn't had any firearms on the premises.

Gathering information for the county council ate up most of Caleb's time. Then, aggravatingly, he didn't turn out to need most of it during the monthly meeting, during which his biggest challenge was maintaining an alert expression for three interminable hours while not developing twitches.

Thursday afternoon, he drove to the Kemps'. He could pretend to be dismayed when he found out Abby had gone to town for her physical-therapy appointment. Easy for him to forget, right? He took a round-about way to be sure he didn't pass the Kemps' buggy.

No sign of Eli or Isaac when he parked. He'd half hoped Nancy would be off visiting and no one at all would be in the house, but she opened the door and greeted him with apparent pleasure. "Sheriff! Come in, come in." When he did so, she switched to Deitsch. "You've missed Abby, if that's who you came to see. Joshua drove her to town to see that man."

He gave himself a light rap on the head. "I meant to offer to drive her again. I've just been so busy…"

"Not so busy you can't have coffee and a bite to eat! I just made dried-apple dumplings."

He smiled at her. "I'm never too busy for *schnitz und knepp.*"

She chuckled contentedly. "I didn't think so."

After dishing up for him, she bustled around the kitchen, not seemingly doing much. He made conversation for a few minutes, conscious of the clock's ticking, then said, "You must have been in the middle of doing something."

"Ach, working in the garden, nothing that can't wait."

Perfect.

He took a last bite and another swallow of coffee. "You go right ahead, Nancy. I'll finish my coffee and let myself out."

She protested, he insisted and she surrendered, leaving him alone in the kitchen.

Alone in the house.

Caleb dumped the rest of the coffee in the sink and quietly headed for the staircase. Now, all he had to do was figure out which room was Abby's.

THE CAR CAME out of nowhere.

Abby had let herself be lulled into a meditative state by the drone of metal wheel rims on pavement, the clip-clop of hooves, the sway of the buggy. She'd slept even less well since the kiss and had assured Joshua she didn't mind if he listened to his iPod. He had shyly showed it to her the first time he drove her to town. It was an old one, but still working.

"Elam Yoder gave it to me," he'd told her. "You know. After he was baptized."

Abby nodded understanding. Electronic devices like an iPod were strictly forbidden for church members, except for telephones necessary to run a business—and then the bishop had to approve them.

"He says Jacob Mast gave it to *him*." Joshua clearly marveled at that, and she knew why. Jacob Mast was now a bearded man with a pregnant wife and two-year-old son, chosen by God to be a minister besides. *Jacob*, listening to who knew what kind of music via an earbud?

Much of the way today, Joshua had steered Sadie Mae, a pretty dark brown mare, along a quiet country road. They could have reached town faster taking the more direct highway as they had Tuesday, but Abby was glad he'd chosen the different route. He and Sadie Mae hadn't seemed to mind the speed with which cars and trucks passed, barely a few feet separating them from the frail buggy, but Abby had jumped each time, her pulse racing until they turned into town.

Now, immersed in her thoughts, she paid no attention to the intersection ahead, not a busy one. Obedient to Joshua, the mare slowed until he clucked and they started across the two-lane road.

The sudden roar of an engine jerked Abby into awareness. A black sedan closed in on them so fast, there was nothing Joshua could do. Even calm Sadie Mae broke her stride. Abby had only an instant to try to brace herself for the impact.

Brakes screeched, but too late. Abby was looking right into the driver's eyes when the crunch came, and the buggy flew sideways. Joshua was yelling something, the horse screamed, but she felt as if time had slowed, as if she was having an out-of-body moment. The steel wheel rims made terrible sounds as they scraped sideways across the pavement. The buggy broke into pieces. Abby realized in a dreamlike way that she lay almost across the shiny hood of the car.

And then they stopped. All of them. The silence was deafening.

The driver's side door opened. She expected to hear the man panicking, saying, *Are you hurt? I've called 9-1-1!* but maybe she'd lost her hearing.

With difficulty, she turned her head to see what had happened to Joshua. To her astonishment, he remained in his seat, although much of the buggy no longer enclosed him. He sat frozen, his mouth open in an O but no sound emerging.

It's me, she thought, except suddenly she *did* hear a man's voice. More, the hum of wheels, the fast *clop-clop* of an approaching horse and buggy. This voice spoke Deitsch, which her mind momentarily didn't want to interpret, but the alarm was evident.

The car door slammed. She once again saw the driver's face through the windshield, his eyes burning into hers. But the car was moving, backing up, the bumper wrenching free from the wreckage with a horrible sound, and she couldn't find any purchase on the slick metal of the hood. She futilely tried to dig her fingers in, but as the man accelerated in reverse, she slid backward and tumbled off, trying to go limp except for cradling her head as the pavement came at her.

Then the car swerved around them and sped off with a screech and the smell of burning rubber, topping a gentle hill to disappear over it.

"WE'RE SO LUCKY you came along!" Abby exclaimed, for what had to be the third or fourth time.

They were lucky, all around. Neither she nor

Joshua were badly hurt, just scraped and bruised. The buggy was history, but Sadie Mae had staggered to her feet and was able to limp slowly up the lane to the nearest farm. The owner, a man named Nick Cobb, wasn't Amish and had appeared with a cell phone in hand. He'd already called the police and was on the phone with a veterinarian by the time Amos King helped Abby and Joshua into the rear seats of his big family buggy to take them home.

Nick Cobb had waved them on. "You don't need to stand around here. The deputy will know where to find you for his report." He'd shaken his head. "Bad enough to hit you, but then to take off."

Hit us on purpose, Abby feared, although anyone else would call her paranoid for thinking so. And… maybe she was. Her throat constricted. Two near misses in a matter of weeks…and this time Joshua could have easily been a casualty as well.

Right now, she hurt all over, and decided she could think about this later. Amos King's buggy rattled and shook its way up the dirt driveway to Eli and Nancy's house, stopping behind a sheriff's-department SUV. Caleb? Why would he be here? Amos secured the reins and came around to help her out. Her knees tried to crumple.

"I think I need to lie down."

"Ja," he agreed, studying her with worry. "I will help you to the house. Joshua, you must wait for me to come back—do you hear me?"

The teenager nodded agreement.

She did lean on Amos's arm until they reached the front door. Inside, she heard someone coming downstairs—Aenti Nancy, Abby thought in relief. The door swung open…but Caleb stood there, looking as shocked as she felt.

HELL. UPSTAIRS WHEN he'd heard voices out front, he'd about had a heart attack. He'd yanked at the duffel zipper, but when it stuck he'd had to abandon it. By the time footsteps sounded on the front porch, he'd made it downstairs in time to swipe the sweat off his forehead with his shirtsleeve. Visitors, he tried to tell himself; he'd have heard a car arriving. But he opened the door to find Abby clutching the arm of a stranger, an Amishman. She'd come so close to catching him red-handed—

He took in what he was seeing. Battered and dirty, *kapp* missing, dress torn and hair wild, she swayed on her feet. "Abby!" He reached for her, looking at the man. "What happened?"

"You are the sheriff, *ja*?"

"Yes."

"There was an accident. I came along just as it happened." His accent was stronger than some. "A car hit the buggy. It was…" He visibly groped for a word. *"Erector."*

"Destroyed."

"Ja."

The images Caleb imagined seemed to tighten a fist around his heart. Abby could have died, he thought, sickened. And he hadn't driven her to her appointment today because he wanted to search her room. "Joshua," he said, remembering suddenly.

The man gestured toward his large buggy. "The Lord was with them," he said simply.

"Did anyone call 9-1-1?"

"*Ja*, a fellow who lives near. Nick Cobb."

"I know Nick." He bent to sweep Abby up in his arms. "I think you should go to the ER."

Something like panic widened her eyes. "I've had enough of hospitals. I just want to lie down. Please."

Caleb frowned down at her, but finally said, "Okay. For now. I'll carry you up, then find Nancy."

She peered at him as if trying to read his thoughts, but said only, politely, "Thank you." She looked back at the stranger who'd brought her home and thanked him, too, in Pennsylvania Dutch.

"It makes no trouble," the man returned politely.

Caleb ended the exchange by starting up the stairs. He carried her straight to her room, which he already knew was spare as a nun's cell, containing only a twin bed and dresser, and pegs on the wall to hang bonnets and capes. The duffle bag sat atop the dresser, and a box of books beside it. He'd flipped through all those books earlier. Now he pulled aside the covers and gently laid her down. After removing her shoes, he sat on the edge of the bed beside her for a minute, unable to stop himself from smoothing back her hair. He found a lump and inspected the bruise forming on her jaw even as his fingertips tingled pleasantly from the silky feel of her skin.

"You're sure nothing's broken?"

Her lashes rose. "No. Really. Will you go help Joshua?"

"Yeah," he said roughly. "Damn." He pushed himself to his feet. "I'll send Nancy up, then find out what happened."

She opened her mouth as if to say something... then closed it.

Caleb kissed her forehead, stroked the uninjured side of her face and left to do his job.

It wasn't until he descended the stairs to find Nancy fluttering around her youngest son that he realized how badly he'd just screwed up. He shouldn't have known which bedroom was Abby's without asking. He could only hope that, stressed, she hadn't noticed.

After getting the story from Joshua, who appeared less damaged than Abby, Caleb talked to the man who'd brought them home. Amos King. He knew the name, but it took a minute for him to remember why. Amos was a furniture maker who had lost his workshop and house to a tornado last year. But in the way of the Amish, within a couple of weeks a new house had been built, with the barn raising shortly thereafter. Other craftsmen within the community, Amish and Englisch, had donated furniture and pieces of art to be auctioned, the proceeds to replace his tools and household goods. A widower, Amos was a good man from all Caleb had heard.

In telling what he'd seen, Amos echoed something Joshua said.

"The place where the accident happened—it is in a dip, I think you say." With his hand, he shaped a roller-coaster track. "I didn't see the car coming over the hill. It must have," he said in puzzlement, "but…" He shook his head.

When Caleb asked if he'd noticed the license plate, Amos only shook his head again. Approaching from the side, he probably wouldn't have seen it, but being Amish he likely wouldn't have paid attention anyway.

Damn, he should have asked Abby about the license plate. She'd surely have looked for one even amidst chaos.

Caleb drove to the site, hoping Nick Cobb could provide another perspective, but when he rolled to a stop behind a deputy's car and got out, he couldn't do anything but stand stock-still, staring in shock at the wreckage.

The torque from the force of the car striking the buggy had ripped the black fiberglass body to pieces. Both the Plexiglas windshield and the splashboard— the buggy equivalent of a dashboard—had broken in half. The steel tire rims were twisted. Bits of glass littered the pavement, just as they did after a typical car accident. The local bishops all encouraged their church members to have battery-operated lights and turn signals on their buggies, unlike in some more conservative districts. The right front light and turn signal both had been smashed.

Pulling himself together with an effort, Caleb exchanged a few words with the two deputies present, then crouched to study the glass. Was there any chance a headlight or other light on the car had broken, too? Unfortunately, he didn't think there was enough glass for both. They'd go over the panels of the buggy with a magnifying glass in hopes of finding a scraping of paint from the car that had hit it. Paint samples could be compared in online databases and lead them to the car make and model. The fact that it had been black, like the buggy, just made their search a little more difficult.

"It's a miracle they survived," he said flatly. He couldn't figure out how they had.

"Maybe there's something to their faith," the older of the two deputies remarked, shaking his head.

Abby wasn't Amish.

A heavy weight in his chest, he turned his back on the wreckage to return to his vehicle.

ABBY LAY IN BED aching as she waited for the ibuprofen she'd swallowed to take effect. She brooded about whether the accident had been just that and, if so, why the man had stared at her with such fury as he reversed the car before fleeing.

There were people who didn't like the Amish, thought them un-American or cultlike, or at least resented having to watch constantly for their slow-moving buggies. He might blame her and Joshua for the accident, be angry because he could be ticketed for speeding if caught, or see a raise in his insurance rates. Still, remembering the hateful glare, Abby shivered.

Finally, she dragged herself up to find fresh clothing to take with her to the bathroom. A hot bath sounded heavenly. Joshua had already taken one; she'd heard the water draining a few minutes ago. Ruefully, she looked down at the dress. It could be mended enough for her to wear for scrubbing floors or weeding the garden, but not for when she'd be seen by anyone outside the family. Her Amish wardrobe had already been limited, and her own sewing skills were pathetic. Aenti Nancy would probably make her a new dress. Given how much taller Abby was than most Amish women, she couldn't borrow.

It took her a minute of looking around to realize neither her *kapp* nor the black bonnet she'd worn were anywhere to be found. Would somebody think to pick them up out of the wreckage, or would they be beyond repair?

Of course, she could put on some of the clothes she'd brought from her real—or, at least, former—life, although she was reluctant to stand out the way she would then. In case someone *was* watching for her.

Her gaze left the dress hanging from a peg to settle on her duffel bag, which she'd never totally unpacked. About all she'd taken out of it were panties and socks, since Amish women didn't wear bras. She'd swear she had left it zipped shut, and now it gaped open. The clothes, at least semineatly packed, were stirred up. A pale pink bra strap had gotten stuck in the zipper.

Surely Joshua wouldn't have been curious enough to poke around in her things. *Somebody* had been…

How dense could she be?

Idle curiosity had nothing to do with it. Her duffel had been searched, and who'd done it was no mystery. The man who insisted he was on her side, who had promised not to lie to her. The man who'd been in the house, seemingly alone, at a time he knew she wouldn't be there.

She couldn't believe she hadn't wondered earlier what he was doing here, wandering around the house.

Feeling angry and, most of all, betrayed, Abby backed away from the dresser and the evidence of what a creep he really was.

Chapter Nine

The instant she saw him, Caleb knew how much trouble he was in.

He'd come back primarily to ask her about the license plate and for any other details she'd recalled. Okay, and to be sure she really was all right.

She sat out on the porch, hands folded in her lap, as if she'd been waiting for him. Which she probably had been. He had to assume she didn't want to talk to him in front of any of her relatives. As he crossed the yard, Abby's face remained expressionless. This was the cop, not the complex woman he'd been getting to know.

Without a word, he sat down and flipped open his notebook on the wide arm of the Adirondack chair. He had to get this out of the way before he let her take her shots.

"Did you see a license plate?"

"There wasn't one in front."

He frowned. "Two are required."

She gave him a did-you-forget-what-I-do-for-a-living look.

"You're sure."

"The car came straight at me. I lay across the hood, slipped off it when the driver backed up. Yes, I'm positive. And no, I did not see the license plate on the back. I should have made an effort, but had other things going on at the time."

Things that had left her with so many visible bruises and scrapes, he hated to think how many more were covered by her stockings and calf-length dress.

"Could it have been covered?"

"No, just not there. I can picture empty screw holes in the bumper."

"Okay. How many people were in the car?" Joshua had thought only the driver, but Caleb had had the impression that the boy had been paralyzed by fear.

"One that I could see."

She closed her eyes when she described the man to him. Unfortunately, she hadn't seen any distinctive features. He'd worn a baseball-style cap with a tractor logo on it that didn't go with the car, which she described as a full-size sedan. He'd worn sunglasses when he first hit them, but they must have fallen off in the collision.

"He was furious," she said calmly. "If looks could kill."

"You're not suggesting this was anything but an

accident." Although he wouldn't be much of a cop if he hadn't already been speculating himself.

"It crossed my mind." Her body language remained placid, her voice willfully calm, her eyes angry. "We should have seen or heard the car coming before we did. I think he was parked on the shoulder in the shade of the grove of trees not that far from the corner. It felt like he was going fast, but if he'd really been at full speed after coming down the hill, I doubt Joshua and I would have survived."

His gut twisted. "The buggy is in pieces."

"I know."

"You didn't recognize the car make?"

"No."

"Anything else you noticed? A bumper sticker, say?"

"No."

After a moment, he closed the notebook and stuck the pen in the spiral-wire top. "Something is on your mind."

"You searched my things."

His jaw hurt, he'd been gritting his teeth so hard. "I…thought it was the one last thing I should do before I told Mike to forget his unlikely scenario."

"I shouldn't be surprised." She stood with a grace that suggested she wasn't feeling any of her pain at the moment. "If we weren't on the porch of my God-fearing aunt and uncle's house, I could tell you what I think of you. As it is, I admit to how gullible I was to believe a single word you ever said."

His chest feeling as though it was being crushed, Caleb rose slowly to his feet. "You can. Abby—"

As if he hadn't spoken, she continued, voice controlled but hard. "This isn't my house, but I'll ask you not to come back, anyway. You have no business with my aunt and uncle, and you have none with me anymore." She walked past him to the door.

"I believe in you," he said to her back.

She kept going. The screen door closed with a slap that stung as if she'd used her hand on his cheek.

"Ach, I need to bake!" Aenti Nancy exclaimed the next morning. "The sheriff is sure to come by—"

"I told him not to," Abby interrupted.

Her aunt turned sharply. "What? Why?"

Feeling hollow, her head dull, she said, "Is Onkel Eli still in the house?" He'd been working on accounts at his antique rolltop desk in the small downstairs office.

"*Ja*, I will get him."

Whether this was right or wrong, Abby didn't know, but she couldn't take any more of her aunt's treating the sheriff as if he was Abby's come-calling friend. He wasn't flirting with her; he was trying to trap her.

Looking worried, her uncle sat down at the kitchen table across from her. Aenti Nancy pulled up the chair beside her. *"Was ist letz?"* he asked.

"You know what happened when I was shot and my partner murdered."

Both nodded. Of course they did.

"I told you that my boss, Sergeant Donahue, believes Neal and I had a falling out and I shot him. I guess the theory is that he got off a couple of shots before he went down."

Nancy began to protest, but her husband silenced her with a glance.

Feeling weary to her bones, Abby continued, "The sheriff already told me that my boss and he had once worked together. That Sergeant Donahue had called and asked him to be friendly to me in hopes I might give something away about whatever awful thing I'd been mixed up in."

"You didn't tell us this, niece." Eli sounded stern.

"I thought—" her voice hitched "—that he had become convinced I was innocent. That he believed me. But yesterday when Amos King brought Joshua and me home, the sheriff was in the house, coming downstairs. I didn't think about it until later, but I found my duffel bag unzipped and everything in it mixed up. When I accused him, he admitted he'd searched my bag, and probably the rest of the room, too."

She saw shock on her aunt's face. Her uncle looked less surprised because he was more aware of the evil the world held.

"I do believe he's good at his job," she said, "that you can trust him if you have need to call the police in the future. But… I can't. I asked him not to come here again. I thought you ought to know why."

After a long silence, Eli nodded gravely. "Un-

less something bad happens, we will not call him."
He pressed his lips together, shook his head. "I had
hoped…"

"Hoped?" Abby prodded.

"That he would help you prove you could never
have done that terrible thing."

"I…suppose I hoped that, too." She tried to smile.
"But Sergeant Donahue is the sheriff's friend, so
it's natural he chose to believe him rather than me."

"I am disappointed," Onkel Eli said heavily, pushing back his hair. "I'm sorry."

"Denke."

When he was gone, Abby squeezed her aunt's
hand. "How is Joshua this morning?" Her body stiff,
she'd come down late enough to miss breakfast.

"Shaken, but excited, too, I think." Aenti Nancy
was clearly dismayed. "He will have something to
tell his friends at the singing Sunday."

Abby laughed. "Ah, to be his age again."

Her aunt didn't move. Abby wasn't accustomed
to seeing her so still. Even during the evening while
Onkel Eli read from the Bible, Nancy knitted or
quilted a small piece in a hoop. She was busy from
the minute she hustled down the stairs until she went
to bed at night. Even given the richness of their diet,
Abby couldn't understand how she stayed stout.

"What will you do?" she asked, lines in her face
Abby didn't remember seeing before. "Once you are
well again. How can you make them believe you?"

"I don't know." The admission made the hollow

inside her expand. "They won't find proof to arrest me, but if nobody else is ever arrested, I can't believe any other police department will be willing to hire me."

"We would be glad if you never left." Her aunt patted her hand and finally stood.

"Denke," Abby said again, forcing a smile, even though she knew that the only way she could stay was to join the church and become Amish in truth, and that wasn't something she could ever do.

CALEB HAD TO TRY. He knocked on the Kemps' door the next afternoon but wasn't surprised when Nancy didn't invite him in. She said, "Abby doesn't want to see you," and closed the door in his face.

This wasn't a good moment to realize he'd fallen completely for Abigail Baker. He had zero chance with her now, but he thought the worst part might be that in destroying her trust, he had left her isolated.

As bleak as he felt, he had to do whatever he could to protect her. Since he was out here anyway, he drove from house to house, both on the Kemps' road and on the one that paralleled theirs, sharing the woods as a greenbelt between properties. The folks on this road were all Amish and presumably knew about Abby. Certainly they'd heard about the buggy accident.

He asked each to watch for strangers lurking in the area, either in cars or in the woods. They weren't in the habit of calling the sheriff's department, but he begged them to make an exception if they saw anything suspicious, especially men they didn't know carrying guns.

Amish landowners were mixed with non-Amish on the next road over. He repeated himself so many times he'd probably mumble the same words in his sleep. Everyone he encountered seemed to be concerned and agreed to watch out for strangers.

To some extent, these rural families would do that anyway. However, since hunting was a way of life for most, the sight of someone passing through with a rifle wouldn't normally occasion any concern. He could only hope that after his warning, they'd be willing to call.

Once back at headquarters, Caleb decided to leave a phone message for Abby, too. Given time to cool off, she might return his call. Knowing his message could well be heard by any of the people who shared the phone kiosk, he had to think about what to say and how to say it.

"Abby Baker, will you sit down with me so I can speak my piece? I want to help, and that's the truth. I can offer resources you need." After a brief hesitation, he added, "Please." That wasn't a word he had intended to use, but he wouldn't have snatched it back if he could.

His phone stayed abnormally silent for the rest of the day. He told himself she probably hadn't gotten the message yet. By lunchtime the following day, he'd given up on that hope.

Midafternoon, a call came in from a local number that he didn't know, which wasn't unusual. His cell phone number did get passed around. He answered, "Sheriff Tanner."

"Sheriff, this is Rudy Yoder. You talked to my son David yesterday." His speech was accented, but clear. "I am calling because you asked. Not an hour ago, my youngest boy and a friend were in the woods behind our place." He paused, as if to be sure Caleb understood what he was saying.

"And what did they see?"

"Two men wearing what looked like military clothing and carrying rifles."

"Camouflage."

"Ja."

Hunters did often wear camo.

"Did the boys talk to them?"

"No, they got frightened. They don't think the men saw them."

"Did you see a car or truck pass by? Or parked?"

"No."

He stifled a sigh. "Thank you for letting me know. I'd recommend you keep the boys out of the woods for now."

"Ja, that's certain sure."

Hearing dead air, Caleb set his phone down. Thinking, he went to the detailed county map that hung on a wall in his office. He'd talked to two different sets of Yoders yesterday; the name was common among the Amish in general, and particularly in this area. There was a good reason for that. At a guess, the first Yoders to come here in search of cheap farmland had likely had eight children, now grown up, married and raising their own families. The first Yoder likely moved with siblings or cousins, too, all buying land in the same area.

At one farm, though, he'd talked to a teenager who said when his *daad* came home, he would tell him to watch for men with guns. It took Caleb a minute to remember where that had been. The picture cleared in his head. The same road as the Kemps, but almost to the end, on the same side.

By the time he got out there, would the men be long gone? The least he could do was hunt for their vehicle.

He drove up and down nearby roads for an hour, failing to find any cars tucked in turnouts or half-covered by shrubbery.

He'd have to trust that Abby was too sore and bruised to do any outdoor work, thus putting herself at risk. Still, he pulled into the Kemps' farmyard. By the time he got out, Eli had appeared from the barn and was walking toward him. Caleb resisted any temptation to look toward the house.

Meeting Eli halfway, he didn't ask if Abby had gotten his message or whether she might be willing to see him. Instead, he said, "I need you to know that not much over an hour ago, Rudy Yoder reported a couple of men wearing camo and carrying rifles in the woods not far from your property. He may have already let you know—"

"He sent one of his boys down."

"Keep an eye out."

Still expressionless, Eli said, "*Ja.* We will do that for sure."

Caleb nodded and left. In the rearview mirror, he saw that Eli hadn't moved beyond crossing his arms. His hat shaded his face.

In the next day and a half, two more reports came in of a man or men carrying rifles lurking in the woods. One caller's description was, "Sneaking around, they were."

Hunting season for turkey opened today, October 1, but it would be another month before deer season opened unless you used a bow and arrow. Pheasant and quail couldn't be hunted until November. You could shoot a squirrel, coyote or groundhog anytime you wanted, but Caleb couldn't quite imagine grown men slinking around in the woods wearing camouflage so they could bag a groundhog. Of course, out-of-season hunting happened. Interestingly, nobody who called had actually heard a gunshot.

A non-Amish caller told him about a vacant piece of property half a mile from his own where a man could park out of sight if he wanted to enter the woods unseen. Caleb once again drove out there, and wished he'd known before that this particular farm was untenanted. The ground was too dry right now to hold a tire track, and the only piece of machinery he saw was an ancient tractor in the barn.

His temper was fraying. Getting back behind the wheel of his SUV, he left the door open while he called Mike Donahue.

"Got something for me?" Mike answered.

"A question."

"Shoot."

Not Caleb's favorite choice of words at the moment. "Do you have someone here in my county watching Detective Baker?"

The pause was just a little longer than Caleb liked before Donahue retorted, "I thought I had *you* keeping an eye on her."

Fuse burning, Caleb let the silence ride.

"You accusing me of something?" Mike sounded pissed.

"Wouldn't think of it." He ended the call before he could say something he'd regret.

Of course, his phone rang twenty seconds later. Mike Donahue. Caleb let it go to voice mail. Then he tipped his head back and tried to think coolly.

Was Abby in danger? He lacked enough evidence to believe she was. On the other hand, she'd had two near misses since she came to stay with her aunt and uncle.

Sure, but the shooting was weeks ago, and the car-buggy collision would be a chancy way to kill someone off…and that's assuming it wasn't an accident, which was a lot more likely. Too many drivers forgot about the likelihood of meeting up with the slow-moving horses and buggies. Or they came from a county or state where no buggy had been seen on the roads in the last century. Here they weren't prepared.

He growled an obscenity, snapped on his seat belt and started the engine.

ABBY PEERED OUT the kitchen window at the sullen sky. Yesterday, a tornado had touched down one county south of them. Nobody killed, thank God, but the Amish grapevine reported plenty of damage to property. Englischer and Amish alike had had homes or barns leveled, fences torn out, dairy cattle killed on one farm, alpacas on another.

She didn't like the color of this sky, or the weight of the air when she'd opened the front door earlier. The leaves on the trees didn't stir; even the ones turning autumn colors didn't fall. The whole world felt too still. Waiting.

She rested her forehead on the glass, admitting that she was having an anxiety attack, and it wasn't tornadoes she feared. She'd never known she was claustrophobic, but that was the closest she could come to describing this feeling. That and helpless, which she hated more than just about anything.

She wasn't supposed to leave the house. She'd had to cancel her physical-therapy appointments for the coming week. She couldn't help Aenti Nancy outside, although the sweet potatoes, tomatoes, pumpkin and squash were coming ripe along with broccoli and cabbage and more beans. She couldn't even dash up to the barn to deliver a message, gather eggs or give grain to either of the harness horses when Eli, Isaac and Joshua were busy with other work.

She was condemned to cleaning house, cooking and helping can the onslaught of ripe produce. This, she thought desperately, was the life of an Amish-woman and could never be hers. The life of a modern young woman didn't always feel like a good fit, either, but being a police officer had satisfied her in a way her Amish relatives would never understand. She could forgive much, but never brutal, senseless violence. That could only be punished.

Caleb would understand. The thought slipped in, however hard she'd been willing herself to keep him out.

He would also understand how her inability to do anything to help *herself* chafed. Coming here had been a mistake, she feared. Now she was stuck. No transportation, no chance to quietly follow the trail of clues Neal had left. No chance to try to compel his wife to talk to her.

Alone in the house, she said out loud, "Why can't I *remember*?" It was all she could do not to yell and hammer her fists on the wall. She wanted to punch Caleb Tanner, because if she'd been able to trust him, he could have helped.

But you can't, so live with it, she told herself coldly. Maybe it was time she returned to her apartment, struck out on her own to investigate. If she took a bus or taxi, no one need know she'd returned to Kansas City. If she was careful, she'd have a while before anyone—say, Sergeant Donahue—knew she was back. Maybe, in familiar surroundings—

Without warning, the familiar pain struck, splintering her brain. Images, sounds, smells glanced off shards of broken glass. Someone crouched over—no, no, no! Footsteps, pain beyond bearing in her head, her hair feeling wet. Blood, had to be blood. Grit on her cheek. Empty holster. Boots. "Hey! I called 9-1-1!" Smell of urine. Someone rearing above her, gun pointing—

Moaning, she staggered to a chair. Bending over, she used the heels of both hands to press her temples until she felt as if a vise held her head together.

"No, no, no, no," she whispered.

She couldn't see the glitter of broken memories anymore. No, not true; they were still there, flickers at the corners of her eyes. If she tried to turn her head, they disappeared.

Slowly the pain eased until she could almost think.

The skip in her brain, the emptiness that was really a wall, was meant to protect her. But if she let it keep protecting her, she wouldn't do a single damn thing to help herself. She had to defy this disability, or she would never be able to move forward with her life.

Unconsciously or not, she'd let herself believe that the detectives in her department were out there seeking answers. That they would do the job she hadn't been able to. She could recover, wait it out until they did make the arrest.

Except she'd lost that faith.

She latched on to the memory of Sam Kirk offering to help...but she couldn't trust him, either.

She thought about the phone message Caleb had left the day before yesterday.

I want to help, and that's the truth. I can offer resources you need. Please.

Onkel Eli had written down every word. She wished she could have heard Caleb's voice so she could judge better what he meant and what was merely a slick attempt to fool her.

Now she was being a fool. How many times had he lied to her? The tenderness of his touch, the passion in his kiss, meant nothing.

Gradually she lifted her head, stretched her back and arms. This attack—how else could she think of it?—had passed. It couldn't have taken as long as it felt, or Aenti Nancy would be back with metal buckets full of beans or a woven basket of cabbages. Abby glanced at the clock, surprised to see how far the minute hand had advanced.

Suddenly worried, she rose to her feet and hurried to the back door. Through the glass, she could see only part of the garden. She opened the door and stepped out, calling, "Aenti Nancy? Are you all right?"

The humidity made it hard to breathe, as if she

was underwater. Her aunt was getting to an age where she shouldn't have to work so hard, lift the heavy baskets of produce the way she did. With this heat, what if she'd fallen, or even had a heart attack?

Abby slipped out, advancing just far enough to see the full sweep of the garden. Aenti Nancy wouldn't have gone up to the barn, would she? And not to the chicken house—she had Joshua gathering…

Oh, thank goodness! There she was in her violet dress and apron, carrying an overloaded basket. Abby called out to her, and Aenti Nancy waved. "Slow, I am! Now, don't you come out."

Except…she stumbled, astonishment on her face.
Crack.

Bullet! Abby's brain screamed.

Aenti Nancy tipped forward in slow motion, ending sprawled on the grass, cabbages tumbled out around her and her sturdy legs bared for anyone to see.

Operating on instinct, Abby ran full out even as she wished desperately for her gun. She dove to cover her aunt, feeling a sudden burn on her upper arm, as if a swarm of hornets had stung her. Stupid, stupid, stupid, but she'd rather die than let any of her family be killed in her place.

Crack. Crack.

A few feet to the compost bin that would offer some protection. But how to drag Nancy there without exposing them even more?

Where were Eli and the boys? *Safe. Please be safe.* She wrapped her arms around her aunt's torso, eased her feet under her…and lunged forward.

Chapter Ten

Caleb got there almost as fast as the ambulance, beating the first responding deputy. He slammed to a stop and leaped out, jogging past the pair of medics grabbing their equipment. *Behind the house,* the caller had said. A shaky young voice, according to the dispatcher.

A cluster of people surrounded the women who were down. Amish except for a boy who hovered a few feet back.

Eli turned his head, probably looking for the medics. His hat was missing, his face wild with fear. "Sheriff. They told you."

"Yes." Caleb looked past him to where Nancy lay stomach down in the dirt by a bin built of slats—compost, he realized. Her *kapp* was blood soaked. Damn, if she'd been shot in the head— "Is she conscious?"

"No." Eli ran a shaky hand over his face. "I must trust in God."

Reminding himself, Caleb thought.

The next second, Caleb realized the second woman was Abby, kneeling at her aunt's side holding her hand. His knees weakened and the tight grip on his lungs loosened. He could breathe again. She was all right.

The paramedics shooed everyone back and began a basic assessment. Nancy didn't even twitch. After scooting a couple of feet, Abby now sat on the bare ground, never looking away from her aunt.

Caleb didn't remember moving, but there he was, squatted at her side, his teeth grinding. "You're injured, too." The sleeve of her dress was soaked with blood.

"It's nothing."

"Abby." He cupped her chin in his hand and turned her face to make her look at him. "It's not nothing. That's a lot of blood. It's dripping off your hand and smeared on your face. *Where do you hurt?*"

He must have roared the question. One of the medics—a woman—swiveled on her heels, obviously assessing Abby.

"Oh, I..." She blinked a few times. "I think a shot grazed my arm, that's all."

She'd been shot for a third time, and it was *nothing*? Caleb couldn't remember ever having been as scared as he was during the drive. The adrenaline cocktail in his body would have ignited a fire if he opened up a vein.

"You need to go to the hospital," he said, with the best semblance of calm he could muster.

For the first time, she looked fully at him. The anguish in her blue eyes did a number on him. "It's nothing compared to—" She gestured helplessly. "If Aenti Nancy dies, it'll be my fault. I should never have come here. I should have—" She started struggling to get to her feet.

Taken off. That's what she wanted to say. "Damn it, Abby." Caleb rose, too, supporting her with an arm around her waist.

A deputy had arrived without his noticing and paused at the back of the ambulance, where the EMTs were about to load Nancy. Eli hovered beside them, anything he said to the deputy distracted. The woman steered him to the front and held open the passenger door. After a minute he nodded and got in.

Caleb looked back down at Abby. "Can you walk?"

"Of course I can." She tried to shake free of him, then seemed to recognize that he wasn't about to release her.

The same medic jogged to them and handed over dressings to Caleb. "Can you bring her to the hospital?" she asked.

"Yes. Go." She took off at a run. Once she leaped in behind the wheel, the siren shrilled and the ambulance started down the driveway.

Joshua and Isaac stared after it, looking very young and scared.

They wouldn't be alone for long, though, Caleb knew. In fact, he saw two Amish women, undoubtedly neighbors who'd heard sirens, moving to one side of the driveway to let the ambulance by, then hurrying toward the small cluster of remaining people. By then, Deputy Booth was already questioning Joshua and Isaac. Isaac was waving his hands in the air and talking when the two women reached them as well.

Caleb let them fuss over Eli and Nancy's sons. The flurry of questions and reassurances might as well have been the chatter of a bird in the branches of the big maple. His attention was entirely on Abby.

He boosted her into the passenger seat of his SUV, then reached to rip her dress.

She gripped his hand. "I can take out some pins."

She did, dropping straight pins into a cup holder, and gingerly lowered the bodice of the dress to pull her arm out of the blood-soaked sleeve. Her cheeks flamed red even under the circumstances, he was stunned to see.

He tore open the packages and used a splash from a water bottle on the first dressing to wipe her arm enough for him to see where the bullet had torn through her flesh. Then he applied the next dressing firmly and said, "Can you hold this? I'll have to grab some tape."

She nodded and laid her hand over it.

Once he'd opened the first-aid kit he always carried and taped the pad to her arm, he said, "Tell me what happened."

Their faces weren't over a foot apart. The last time they'd been this close, he'd been about to kiss her.

Bad timing for the thought to even cross his mind. Maybe fortunately, his question renewed her anguish.

Her throat worked. "I realized Aenti Nancy had been outside a long time." She described what happened from her perspective in a few short words, ending with, "He wasn't a very good shot."

She was right; the shooter certainly hadn't been sniper trained. But since she hadn't seen him, he must have been nearly a hundred yards away. Caleb would find where the man—or men, if the two the boy had seen two days ago had anything to do with this—had set up.

"How many shots were fired?" he asked.

Her forehead crinkled while she thought. Her fingers twitched one by one, as if she had to count on them. "One that brought down Aenti Nancy, then two more when I ran out." She glanced at her arm. "At least two more while I pulled her behind the compost bin. I think one of them hit the compost. The whole bin kind of jumped. There're at least a couple bullets embedded in the house wall, too."

"Okay." He couldn't help himself. He ran his knuckles over her cheek, along her jaw. Silky, warm, and the way her pupils dilated gave him hope.

But the way she looked at him in perplexity, she might not even have noticed his touch. "I don't understand. Why did they stop shooting?"

He glanced over his shoulder, locating the one

person who looked out of place here. "I think we can thank that kid over there. He has to be the one who called 9-1-1. Apparently, he was cutting through the woods and saw and heard enough to get an idea that something bad was happening. He yelled at the shooter to stop, said he had a gun. He fired it once into a tree trunk to show that he meant business, and heard someone crashing away."

"He's not Amish."

"No."

"One of those shots I heard must have been his."

"Maybe." He made himself lower his hand to his side. "I'm going to ask one of my deputies to drive you to the hospital. I need to stay here." However much he hated the idea of letting her out of his sight.

"Okay." She began to squirm forward, but he stopped her with a hand on her shoulder.

"No, we'll just switch vehicles for the moment. You stay put."

Minutes later, he watched as his youngest deputy, a twenty-two-year-old named Caden Vogl, drove away with Abby. Then, as always, he turned to take charge of an investigation that mattered too much to him.

THE MINUTE AN orderly met the police car in front of the ER, Abby blurted, "My aunt, she was just brought in here. Do you know how she is?"

The stocky man raised his brows. "That's a lot of blood. I need you to sit in this wheelchair." Not until she followed his order did he ask, "She came in an ambulance?"

"Yes!"

"I saw them arrive. I don't know any more."

"My uncle must be here—" As the orderly wheeled her into the waiting room, she spotted him. "Onkel Eli!"

He jumped to his feet and hurried to her. Worry had aged his face by a decade. In Deitsch, he said, "Abby, I thought you'd be here sooner. What happened?"

"Nothing. The sheriff sort of patched me up. I'm not hurt badly." Although the pain was starting to make itself felt. "But Aenti Nancy... Have they told you anything?"

"They're moving her to intensive care. Someone is to come and get me. They said the bullet bounced off her head, and they think she will wake up soon, God willing, but she hasn't yet."

She gripped his hand, too close to tears. "I'm sorry. So sorry. This never would have happened if I hadn't come to stay with you, or if I'd left after the first shooting. I should have! I—"

He shook his head. "The person who shot you and Nancy, he must have this on his conscience. Nothing is your fault. What happened today is God's will—you know that, niece."

She couldn't be that accepting. Since her mother had been taken from her, Abby had never lost the burning coal of anger. Mostly, that anger was channeled at the killer, who had escaped justice, but she could not accept that the murder was God's will. She wouldn't have become a cop if she hadn't felt, with a passion her Amish family would never understand, that police could and did prevent such tragedies. Most of the time, they gave resolution to the survivors. She needed to be part of that, not live her life placidly accepting that brutal deaths and the suffering of crime victims might have a greater purpose.

She declined his offer to come with her, insisting he be available so that he could be at Nancy's side the second they'd allow it.

Once she was established in a cubicle, a nurse came in, winced at the sight of her arm, then winced again when she saw the vividly red scar on the same shoulder. "That looks recent. You're having a run of bad luck."

Abby smiled weakly. "You could say that."

Once she'd been cleaned up, the doctor appeared. After a quick look, she offered to call for a plastic surgeon, but Abby shook her head. "What's one more scar?"

The doctor, a middle-aged woman, eyed her. "Is someone gunning for you?"

"Actually…yes. I'm… I was a detective with the Kansas City Police Department before I had to take time off to recuperate. It would seem my last investigation has followed me."

"Do our local police know?"

"Yes, I've been working with Sheriff Tanner."

Now, there was a euphemism. Fighting with him… kissing him…spitting in his face…

"Good." Seeming satisfied, Dr. Henson dressed the wound and gave her instructions as well as prescriptions for antibiotics and painkillers. "Is someone waiting to drive you home?" she asked.

"I don't know." She explained about her aunt and discovered that Dr. Henson had seen Aenti Nancy initially, too.

"Heads are hard," she said. "I worked in an ER in St. Louis for years, so I can tell you head shots seem like a sure thing on TV but aren't so easy to make. The skull curves. Bullets tend to ricochet off, thank heaven."

That was one of the reasons police officers were taught to shoot for the torso if they had to pull the trigger.

Now if only Aenti Nancy would regain consciousness. *With* her memory intact.

THEY'D DUG BULLETS out of the house walls as well as one that had drilled into the ground after penetrating the rich dark compost. After finding the blind, Caleb had scooped one forgotten shell into an evidence bag. A tech was trying to make a cast of the best of several footprints that weren't very revealing, given that the soil was hard and dry at this time of year. They did know that the shooter wore a men's size ten-and-a-half shoe. If a second man or woman had been there, he or she hadn't left a trace.

Best scenario would be finding a fingerprint on the shell. People did get careless. Caleb would celebrate if that happened. Otherwise, the least damaged bullet might conceivably match up with one used in another crime on the database maintained by the ATF. Unfortunately, most of those matches didn't go anywhere, because no arrest had been made in the previous crime. Still…it would be helpful to know what other crimes the shooter had committed and where they had happened.

Yeah, and Caleb was trying to be cool when *enraged* was closer to the mark.

Having been directed to the ICU in the small hospital, he saw a woman wearing faded green scrubs sitting alone in the waiting room. His brain had to shift gears when he recognized Abby, her bright blond hair caught in a high ponytail instead of covered by a *kapp*. Not Amish. His gaze caught on the thick white gauze wrapping her upper left arm. The reminder didn't do anything to help him regain his equilibrium.

Staring at the double doors leading into the ICU, she didn't so much as turn her head when he approached. Not until he sat down beside her did she blink and look at him.

"How's Nancy?" He sounded rusty.

"She's going to be okay." Her smile might have wobbled, but it was real nonetheless. "The bullet ricocheted. She's concussed—what a surprise—but awake and talking. She even remembers seeing me poking my head out the back door and thinking I'd promised not to do that."

"And she's right."

Abby's smile went away. "I should have just left her lying out there?"

"They shot her to create bait. Which you swallowed, hook, line and sinker."

Her knuckles showed white where she gripped the arms of the chair. "They might have shot her again, just to be sure I got the message. I'd rather have died than let her die."

Now he was flat-out furious. "You think that's what *she'd* want? What Eli would want? What *I* could live with?"

Her eyes narrowed. "What do you have to do with it?"

"Plenty," he said from between bared teeth. He wasn't about to tell her he'd been falling like a rock for her since they first met, not when they shared a hospital waiting room with half a dozen other people, a couple of whom he knew.

Abby snorted. "Gee, don't tell me. You've actually come around to believing someone is trying to kill me?"

This was a make-or-break moment. "Abby." He waited until she met his eyes. "I never doubted someone tried in that alley. I've known Donahue long enough, I had to give some credence to his suspicions." When her mouth opened, Caleb held up a hand. "Searching your stuff was my last option. I did it so I could call him and say, *You're wrong*. You've taken ten years or so off my life since you got here. You have to know how I feel about you."

Color blossomed on her cheeks. Gazing into her clear blue eyes, he quit thinking. No, not true. The word *beautiful* was in there, as was *shy*. Which threw him back to her serious blushing when she had to expose a little of her body. It made him wonder—

"I...don't," she whispered.

Don't what? Oh. Know how he felt.

He sneaked a glance around, to find that five of the six other people in the waiting room were watching them. Pretty blonde, cop in uniform—of course they were.

Keeping his voice low, he said, "I assume you're not in a relationship."

"No."

"If you'll give me a chance, you are now."

Her head snapped back. The color in her cheeks brightened, became...angry? "I've given you chances. I did trust you, and you stomped on my trust. Ground it into nothing. How can you possibly imagine I'll, what, bat my eyelashes and say, *Oh, you'll protect me*? Or fall into your arms? Really?"

The woman knew how to hit. "Abby," he started, without knowing what he was going to say. He didn't get a chance to say anything.

"Abby!" It was Eli, who had burst through the double doors. "Nancy wants to talk to you, and the nurse says it's fine. Only one of us in there at a time."

She jumped to her feet and threw her good arm around her uncle. "Thank God she wasn't hurt worse."

"*Ja*, thank God," he whispered against that blond hair.

For a moment they stayed that way, an unlikely pair despite the similarity in coloring. Solid Amishman with wheat-colored hair and a long beard, wearing broadfall denim trousers, sturdy work boots and suspenders stretched in a Y over his back, covered by a blue shirt. Englisch woman in green scrub pants that hugged her curvy hips and showcased amazing legs, V-neck scrub top that bared a long line of throat and some pale chest. And yet, despite their differences, nobody could miss the love.

Caleb had the rare experience of feeling his eyes sting.

The two separated, and Abby's gaze glanced off him as if he were a stranger who happened to be sitting nearby. She turned and hurried across the waiting room and pushed through the doors, leaving Eli to slump into the seat beside Caleb.

"So blessed we are," he said after a minute. His eyes were the exact shade of blue as Abby's, Caleb couldn't help noticing.

Normally, Caleb might have said, *Yeah, we got lucky today.* But he didn't waste his breath. Eli would never see it that way, and right this minute, Caleb wasn't so sure he did, either. Every once in a while, he'd have the thought that Abby could so easily have died in that alley. Given her injuries, it was damn near a miracle that she *hadn't* died. He might never have met her.

Never had the crap scared out of him every week or two, he thought ruefully.

"We are blessed," he agreed. Looking toward the double doors, he said, "Although apparently I'm not blessed enough to be forgiven."

"Abby?" Eli sounded surprised.

Who else? "She isn't willing to believe that I'm on her side." He moved his shoulders to release tension. "That I care about her."

"Do you?" Eli's voice was mild, his eyes—Abby's eyes—less so.

"I do." He'd never said those words in quite that way. "I'd do anything for her, but she doesn't want to let me."

Eli patted his forearm, as if he were one of Eli's sons. "Abby understands that God expects us to forgive one another, just as He forgives us our mistakes. *Ja?*"

"*Ja.* Yeah."

"She will remember that you come to help whenever we need you."

Would she? Caleb smiled crookedly at her uncle. "You know she blames herself for Nancy being hurt."

"*Ja*, she did say that. I reminded her that she takes too much on herself."

"Was she convinced?"

Eli chewed that over for a minute, then sighed. "My niece, she is…" He hesitated.

"*Agasinish,*" Caleb reminded him. The Pennsyl-

vania Dutch word nicely summed up his estimation
of a significant portion of her personality: contrary,
self-willed. Qualities he admired, but ones that were
currently working against him.

Eli chuckled. "*Ja*, that is Abby." His expression
dimmed. "After losing her mother, she struggled to
find a place for herself."

"Why didn't her father give her that?" Caleb
asked.

Eli hesitated long enough, Caleb didn't think he
was going to answer, but he finally did.

"I think my sister was his framework, like with a
good, sturdy barn or house, ain't so? With her killed
the way she was, he became…empty. The one bless-
ing was that he often sent Abby here to us."

"Because of you, she knew she was loved."

"I hope that is so," he said, sounding troubled.
"With these troubles, she may think she doesn't belong with us. Family should be with you when you
need them most, and Abby—" Eli shook his head in
sorrow "—she doesn't want to let anyone else carry
any of the weight. You see?"

He saw.

Damn, what was he going to do? Caleb didn't see
her mood softening in the next couple of hours. She'd
feel better once her aunt was home again. He could
wait a day or two.

NANCY WAS RELEASED the following day, a Tuesday.
From the report Caleb heard, she was in good spir-

its and thwarting every effort to treat her like an invalid. He imagined her heading straight for her kitchen and starting dinner as if nothing had happened. Of course, Abby's stubbornness might be a match for her aunt's. Caleb wouldn't have minded being a witness.

He'd decided to give it one more day, though, before he tried to regain at least an inch or two of lost ground with Abby.

Wednesday, shortly after lunch, he sat behind his desk scowling as he flipped through monthly reports, including claims for overtime.

A ring on the internal line interrupted his brood. "Tanner here."

"A Mr. Kemp is here to see you," the receptionist/dispatcher said. "He says it's important."

Eli, here? "I'll be right down." Caleb moved fast, imagining Abby dead, or having been kidnapped, or—

When he pushed through the doors into the waiting area, he found Eli pacing restlessly, still wearing his summer-weight straw hat.

"Eli?"

The Amishman swung around, his agitation obvious. "It is Abby," he blurted. "She came to town with me. Nancy had a list for me to take to the store. Abby needed clothes. I shouldn't have agreed to bring her, but she rode inside the buggy, where no one could see her. She went into the store with me, but…when I was done, I couldn't find her."

Caleb's hands curled into fists. "Somebody took her?"

"No. She ran away." Eli thrust a crumpled piece of paper at him. "This was on my seat in the buggy."

With dread, Caleb read the brief note.

If I don't leave, bad things will keep happening. I brought my debit card with me so I'd have money, and caught a bus. If you spread the word that I'm gone, that would be good. Thank you for taking me in. I love you both.

Caleb ground his teeth together. She'd drive him insane. Did she really think he'd let her go off on her own with a killer on her heels?

Chapter Eleven

Still dressed as an Amishwoman, Abby had several rows to herself on the swaying bus. That was just chance—for longer journeys, the Amish often took buses, and to locals there'd be nothing remarkable in the sight of her traveling.

Nobody had appeared to be paying attention when she got on outside the Amish Café on the main street, right behind an Englisch woman with two young children. Wearing a black bonnet, Abby had kept her head down and face averted from the few passersby before the bus pulled in. Thank goodness Onkel Eli hadn't come out of Ralph's General Store too soon!

Now she gazed out a grimy window across the westbound lane of the highway at farmland and scattered houses and barns. Those belonging to the Amish were easy to pick out, since no electrical wires connected their homes or workshops to the lines strung between poles on the highway. In the world, but not of it—that was their way. Abby couldn't help feeling an ache in her chest as she saw an Amish farmer plowing under the stubble left from corn, a team of four draft horses pulling willingly. That man, with his broad back and strong arms gripping the plow, could have been her uncle.

Shaking off emotions she couldn't afford, she again studied the bus schedule she'd brought with her. She'd already decided that instead of remaining on this bus as it ambled its way east toward the Mississippi River and the town of Hannibal, she'd hop off in Day's Creek, the upcoming town, and take a different bus that was supposed to stop there twenty minutes later. What she hadn't decided yet was whether, given that twenty minutes, she ought to whisk into a restroom and pull the dress over her head and unroll the jeans she wore beneath it, transforming herself instantly into an Englisch woman, or whether it would be safer to stay Amish for a while. She *would* be noticed if she used an ATM while wearing a dress and bonnet, and her cash would run low soon. No matter which she did, Abby planned to keep switching buses, confusing any tail as much as possible.

She'd considered calling Julie Luong, her friend at the police department, but anyone who knew much about her would expect that, even start keeping an eye on Julie once Abby's disappearance became known. Ditto for Dad, of course. And who else was there?

An annoying, persistent voice whispered a name. She did her best to shut it down. The next-to-last time she'd seen him, he'd been searching her bedroom for information he could turn over to Donahue.

No. Just...*no*.

Several vehicles had passed the bus, drivers frustrated at the turtle's pace that seemed to be its top speed. She'd tried to get a peek at them before leaning forward as if she'd dropped something on the floor. It was paranoid to think anybody would already be after her, but just in case, she'd ensure she wasn't seen until she had get to out at the bus stop.

For a moment, she rested her head back and closed her eyes, taking long, slow breaths in an effort to conquer nausea she blamed on diesel fumes and the swaying, bouncing ride. Something cold to drink would be good. She could take the time to buy a soda, unless the stop wasn't near enough to a store.

Her thoughts flew a hundred ways. She imagined the icy-cold can of soda with droplets of condensation. Caleb's face when she walked away from him in the hospital. What Onkel Eli would do when he found the note. The tenderness in Caleb's touch when she was hurt. Always, she returned to the danger stalking her.

Was someone determined to kill her only because he feared she recognized him as he bent over her in the alley? Or did he know she hadn't seen him and was instead afraid Neal had confided in her, that she would soon remember what her partner had told her? She puzzled at that for a few minutes. Maybe Neal *had* told her in the days leading up to the shooting.

If so, that information was locked in the closed vault of her unrecoverable memories.

There must be a way to dynamite that lock, free everything hidden behind the door.

Flick. Her mind took off in a new direction.

Caleb would be mad when he heard that she was gone.

She wanted so much to trust him. Abby couldn't forget the sheer relief of resting against his tall, powerful body. Nobody had held her in such a very long time, and never quite the way he did. She'd never felt even close to the way she had when he kissed her, either.

She steeled herself against the likelihood she'd never see him again. A part of her wanted to believe he'd call her, or even show up on her doorstep, once this was all over. But that was just foolish.

Movement seen in the corner of her eye gave her barely a second to duck below the level of the window. A black SUV—but they were so common here, along with pickup trucks.

Damn it, she had to get over letting *everything* make her think of him.

She made herself envision the can of soda again. The sound when she popped the top, the rush of cold liquid and bubbles and caffeine that would be her first swallow.

The bus was slowing down, the typical small town appearing ahead. Brakes squealed as they lumbered toward an unwieldy stop at the curb in front of a store called E & W Foodstop. No, the bus rolled forward just a little more, and Abby could see into the windows of a diner.

As the front doors flapped open, she gathered her cloth bag and stepped into the aisle. Only two of them getting off here. Hiding beneath the brim of her bonnet, she nodded at the driver as she passed and said a shy, *"Denke."*

Once onto the sidewalk, she moved into the narrow band of shade cast by a roof overhang and waited until the bus lumbered on its way again before starting toward the convenience store.

Because she was a cop, she saw the young man who'd also gotten off the bus hopping into the bed of a beater of a pickup truck with a muffler issue. Not safe, but this wasn't her jurisdiction. On a tiny shock, Abby reminded herself that she didn't *have* a jurisdiction.

Across the street, a woman was outside washing the plate-glass front windows of a florist. A couple juggling grocery bags emerged from the grocery store and disappeared around the corner of the building into what Abby guessed was a parking lot beyond it.

An old Cadillac that must be a gas hog passed. On her side of the street, a red van approached, slowed, looked like it was either going to turn into the parking lot or pull up to the curb.

She was twenty feet from the door into the store when the van accelerated and slammed to a stop beside her. A side door slid open and a man leaped out. Abby spun, tried to run, but she didn't make two steps before a meaty arm locked around her neck while a hand slapped over her face.

CALEB HAD BEEN hovering in the alcove surrounding the glass doors into the grocery store. Having caught up with the bus and passed it only a mile or so out of town, he'd parked in the store lot, asked the first person he saw where the bus stopped and then found the best place to lurk.

He got some looks, but that wasn't unexpected given that he wore his uniform, as he did most days. A few people smiled when he held open the door for them. He hoped Abby did get off here, because Day's Creek contracted with the sheriff's department for police services. If he had to take Abby Baker into protective custody, at least here he could do it legally.

Once the bus arrived, he weighed whether to get on it as soon as the doors opened and haul her ass out or follow on to the next town. Before he could decide, he saw an Amishwoman rise and start down the aisle. Was this her idea of being tricky?

The approaching van was the kind people bought to ferry a herd of kids to school, activities and friends' houses. A mom van. Caleb watched it, anyway, expecting it to turn into the parking lot. At the same time, he automatically clicked on details that felt wrong. The driver was male, not female, and another man sat in the back. When the van leaped forward, Caleb took off running.

He'd closed half the distance by the time a man dressed in black with a ski mask over his face snatched Abby. Her bonnet wrenched askew, she wouldn't be able to see much of anything. But she fought anyway. Her knee came up to let her stab a foot backward. Her assailant staggered but didn't release her.

And then Caleb reached them. He ripped the bastard off Abby, flung him to the sidewalk. She'd gone to her hands and knees but immediately jumped up. The second guy had gotten out and made it to the sidewalk by then. Instead of wading in to help his partner, he grabbed her.

"Knife!" she yelled, before kneeing this one in the exact right place.

Caleb spun to one side. The sting on his upper arm said he'd reacted barely in time. Facing off with ski-mask guy, he focused on the knife, black from hilt to tip of the blade. KA-BAR, or a knockoff. Behind him, he heard Abby screaming in rage and some clangs off metal.

He'd pulled his Glock often enough to do it in a split second. "Put the knife down."

The creep flung himself toward the van, yelling, "Go! Go!"

Caleb whirled. "Freeze!"

Time shifted into slow motion. The one with his hands on Abby let her go and threw himself in the side door of the van. She fell hard. The other SOB was already behind the wheel. The van burned rubber accelerating away from the curb. Caleb would have shot out the tires, but risked hitting somebody. A couple of dozen people had come out of businesses on both sides of the road to gape. A car approached.

If it hadn't been for Abby, he'd have pursued. But this time, she wasn't getting up, which decided for him.

He dropped to his knees, saw that she was conscious, holstered his gun and yanked out his phone. Since he'd taken in the model and maker of the van as well as the license-plate number, he issued a BOLO on it.

Then he carefully untied the strings under her chin that held the bonnet on her head and pushed it away. The *kapp* went with it.

"You're hurt," he said hoarsely. Hurt again, because he hadn't been fast enough. Because she'd been an idiot. He had no trouble blaming both of them for this fiasco.

"I...don't think so. I landed on my bad shoulder and arm, and... I'm catching my breath, that's all."

He swore and let his head fall forward. "You can't keep doing this to me."

"But you keep doing this for me."

Something in her voice persuaded him to lift his head, to look at her face, where he saw that her lips had curved into an uncertain smile.

She struggled to a sitting position with his help. So far, he'd ignored the crowd of people encircling them.

"What can we do?" asked a middle-aged man in twill cargo pants and heavy-duty work boots.

Caleb rose to his feet. "I'd ask if anybody recognized those men, except, well…"

"Bet they were sweating under those masks," another man commented, nodding toward the bank a half a block down. It showed time and a ninety-seven-degrees-Fahrenheit temperature.

"Safe to say."

"Well, I recognize the van," a woman said indignantly. "Didn't you see the bumper sticker?"

He had. Bright yellow and black, it said HOME-SCHOOL BUS.

Abby started to laugh.

Until the man who'd first spoken said, "Sheriff, you do know you're bleeding."

THE GENERAL PRACTITIONER who was apparently the only doctor in town hustled both Abby and Caleb in, leaving some wide-eyed folks there for appointments waiting in front.

"You're bleeding," the nurse said briskly. "They're not."

Abby had scrapes on her knees, her elbow, the heels of her hands and her jaw. The nurse cleaned them up, applied something that stung and had Abby emitting squeaks, and applied gauze where needed. When she finished, the nurse said, "Now, I know you folks don't carry insurance or probably money with you, so here's what we'll do."

Abby smiled. "I'm actually not Amish. Well, I've been visiting Amish family, which is why—" She gestured at herself. "And even though I do have insurance, I'll just pay."

Belatedly, she wondered if she did still have health insurance. Something she needed to look into, especially the way things were going lately. She'd pay whatever was necessary to hold on to it until…well, until.

The nurse showed her across the hall to where the doctor was working on Caleb. Abby walked in without thinking. At the sight of his bare torso, she froze and all she could do was stare. It wasn't as if she hadn't seen shirtless men plenty of times, from high school to police locker rooms. But this was Caleb, and he was…beautiful. Perfect. Well-defined muscles rippled under lightly tanned skin and chest hair a shade darker than the sun-streaked bronze on his head. Washboard abs, strong throat when she lifted her gaze…and finally met his eyes, which had a glint that meant he'd been watching her. It took getting a little dizzy for her to realize she'd quit breathing. She sucked in some air and tried to sound nonchalant. "Sorry, I thought you'd be through."

"Almost there," said the doctor cheerfully. He sat on a rolling stool, his bushy white hair a match to the white lab coat. "Had to put in a few stitches."

A *few*? Abby's chest cramped as she studied the line of stitches circling his left bicep.

"Fourteen," the doctor added.

Caleb grimaced. "I've had more."

"So I see."

Abby saw, too: the white line of an old scar crossing his rib cage at an angle. That had to have been a knife, too.

This time, though, it was—

"If you say this is your fault," he growled, "I swear I'll grab that tape and use it to shut your mouth."

The doctor's eyebrows shot up, but Abby found in herself the ability to laugh.

"Well, it *is* my fault, and you can try."

Caleb smiled and held out his right hand. She took the few steps around the exam table to put her hand in his and exchange comfort.

A minute later, Dr. Sanford finished and made a pleased sound, told them the nurse would be in to apply a dressing and give him prescriptions, and whisked out.

"I think I have the same instructions from my last GSW," Abby said. "I could just share them."

Caleb didn't look amused. "Did those instructions mention your suggested activity level? Say, not getting into a fight for your life?"

"Uh, I don't think there was anything that specific." Although she'd been cautioned not to lift heavy weights with that arm, or lift it higher than her shoulder. No wonder it hurt.

Once the nurse had done her part, they went out front to settle their bills and then, after he took a cautious look outside, got into Caleb's department SUV.

He put the key in the ignition, then let his hand drop back to his thigh.

"A deputy found the van abandoned half a mile down the highway, within walking distance of where it was stolen."

She nodded acknowledgment, not looking at him. "I can't go back to my aunt and uncle's."

"I have no intention of taking you there."

"Could you drive me somewhere I could safely hop a different bus? They'd never find me."

"Not a chance," he said flatly, finally starting the engine. He released the emergency brake, checked over his shoulder and backed out.

"It makes sense," she argued.

At an angle in the parking lot, he braked hard, then glared at her. "Sense? What are you going to do? Ride buses for the rest of your life? Hole up in the woods somewhere, off the grid? Are you a hunter, Abby? Or, let me think, maybe you intend to settle back at home?"

Home. She had the unsettling sensation of just having gone over a speed bump. Kansas City, her apartment there, wasn't home. Had it ever been? Did she truly have a home?

"I need to retrace Neal's steps." Her fingernails bit into her palms. "I'll never be safe until I know why he had to die."

"And how long do you think you'll live once you stick your nose out there asking questions?"

Oh, he was mad. Well, so was she.

"I've waited way too long for someone else to fix this!" she yelled. "You and your BFF Donahue aren't any use, since you're fixated on me. I can't trust anybody in the department. And what were you doing here today, anyway? Hoping I'd lead you to my coconspirators? And then, heck, they tried to abduct me instead. What a disappointment."

Jaw hard, he said, "Are you done?"

"For the moment." She set her mouth mutinously.

"I followed because I was afraid for you." His voice was quiet. So quiet, she felt shame creep over her. She knew why he'd been here in the nick of time today, and it had nothing to do with suspecting her.

"I know," she mumbled, gazing at her gauze-wrapped palms. He had betrayed her trust in one way, but she'd always known he wouldn't hurt her, or allow anyone else to hurt her.

"You ready to listen to me?"

Her head bobbed.

"We'll give ourselves a day or two, then *we'll* retrace your partner's steps. While being very, very careful."

Humiliated at the burning in her eyes, Abby lifted her head. "What about Donahue?"

"What about him?"

"Will you tell him what we're doing?"

"No."

"Okay," she said after a minute. "I don't think I've said this yet, but thanks. I mean, for following me today."

He bent his head and kissed her, so softly she started to melt. But he straightened before she could lift a hand to that hard cheek. He barely paused before turning out of the clinic lot.

Abby let him drive in silence for at least five minutes before she had to ask, because trust only went so far.

"Where are you taking me?"

Caleb flicked a glance at her. "Home with me."

Stunned, she said inanely, "Your...house?"

He didn't crack a smile. "Yeah."

"But..."

"But what? You'll be safe there. And in case you're wondering, no, you don't have to share my bed."

"I wasn't!" Was she?

"Then what's your objection?"

She came up with a big blank. A whiteboard scrubbed clean. That was the moment when Abby realized there was no place in the world she'd rather go than home with Caleb Tanner.

So she took a deep breath and told him, "I don't have an objection."

"Good." He took one hand off the wheel to take hers in a warm, reassuring clasp that made her too warm and...excited.

Chapter Twelve

School must have let out for the day, because two teenage boys were shooting baskets in a driveway across the street, while several younger boys rode bikes over a low plywood jump on a sidewalk. A toddler girl watched wistfully from her seat on a plastic big-wheel trike from a nearby lawn.

Abby let the drape fall back into place, leaving her in the dimly lit living room. The house was awfully quiet, and she didn't know what to do with herself. Caleb had left her because he needed to check in at headquarters and then take a run out to her aunt and uncle's place to pick up her duffel bag with another change of clothes in it as well as her books.

Not that he didn't have books aplenty, as she'd already discovered.

He'd shown her to a guest room upstairs in his home, a two-story she guessed dated to 1910 or so. It had wonderful woodwork, gleaming oak floors, a carved fireplace mantel that had been restored and a dining room with built-in glass-fronted buffet. She all but tiptoed as she explored. She knew he wouldn't mind—the last thing he'd said was *Make yourself at home*—but there was a fine line between acting like a guest and being flat-out nosy. The thing was, she could tell a lot about someone from his living quarters, and Caleb remained too much of an enigma to her. For example, while she had faith that he didn't currently have a girlfriend, had he ever been married? Did he have children? Had he really meant it when he said that he wanted a relationship with her? And what did *that* mean? Just sex, or more?

"Aagh!" She could drive herself nuts. *Was* driving herself nuts. *So go explore.* He'd never know if she didn't touch.

The kitchen was the one room in the house that must have been remodeled from the studs out. The cabinets were oak and fit the age of the house, but she suspected they were new. When she tentatively opened a drawer, it slid like silk. The appliances had to be new, too. An alcove held an antique round oak table, the small-paned windows covered with filmy white curtains.

Tucked in a small room at the back of the house was a businesslike office that included a laptop computer and printer on the desk and old-fashioned oak file cabinets. She barely peeked in there, because poking around on his computer or paperwork *would* have been intruding.

Next to the office was what was euphemistically called a powder room. Upstairs—despite her attempt to step lightly, as several steps creaked underfoot—she already knew there were two full bathrooms: one she'd have to herself, the other presumably attached to Caleb's bedroom. Now she opened doors, finding a linen closet that she guessed had been carved out of the guest bedroom. It was furnished, but Spartan, with cream-colored walls, a queen-size bed, a dresser and a closet that wouldn't have been original in a house of this era.

Opening doors, she found two empty bedrooms. The door to his stood ajar. His room was plain enough to have pleased an Amishman, with no artwork or wallpaper on the walls. Antique dresser, walk-in closet, door opening into—yes—a bathroom with a claw-footed tub, and a giant bed covered by an Amish quilt, a log-cabin pattern in shades of green.

It was really hard to look away from that bed. Especially now that she knew what he looked like after he pulled off his shirt.

She loved everything about the house, and especially this bedroom. It suited him, she decided. She didn't see a hint that this was a man who missed the big city, nightlife, a risky job.

Abby moaned, went to the guest bedroom and decided to lie down. Not that she'd fall asleep.

Eyes closed, she imagined climbing into his bathtub, filled with hot water. Maybe some bubble bath. She hadn't actually taken a bubble bath since she was a little girl, but this was her fantasy. Besides, she could hide beneath the bubbles if Caleb should happen to open the door and walk in… Floating in her imagined bath, she began to drift.

CALEB HAD BEEN eager to come home in a way he didn't ever remember being. When he walked in the kitchen door to silence, worry took root. Could he have been followed when he drove her here? He'd swear not, but—damn it, she wouldn't have taken off again, would she? He should have been suspicious of her ready agreement to his plan.

"Abby?"

No answer. He took the stairs two at a time, trying not to make too much noise in case she was here and napping. He had to brace himself before he eased her door open enough to see the bed.

The punch of relief when he saw her curled up sound asleep took him aback. She'd had him on a roller coaster, all right, although she was on it, too, a few cars ahead of him. If they could sit in the same car, he'd be a lot happier.

He walked quietly into the room to look down at her. In sleep, she was softer, unable to guard her expressions. He was reminded of how fine-boned she was, and disturbed anew by the gauze wrapping her hands and the raw scrape on her jaw. She'd been repeatedly wounded, although at least this time he'd been there to step in. Not that she hadn't fought viciously, but if it had been two against one, and with her unarmed, Caleb figured they'd have succeeded in stuffing her into the van. She wouldn't have lived long.

It was the *why* of all this that ate at him. If she and her partner had surprised a drug dealer doing business, say, he'd gotten away with murdering one cop and injuring another. How much could she realistically have seen in the dark behind the bar? So what if her memory returned?

And an even bigger question: How did the shooter know she'd lost her memory and therefore hadn't been able to give testimony yet? How did he know where she'd gone after being released from the hospital?

Why was she such a threat?

The answer had been staring him in the face all along, of course. She was a threat because she knew the shooter. Because she would have recognized him.

That could have been because she'd arrested him before, or because he was one of the people she and the partner had talked to in the weeks before the shooting. That left the problem of how this hypothetical bad guy got confidential information from her doctor, or how he'd learned where she had gone after being released.

Caleb had been reluctant to admit even to himself the obvious answer.

She'd been shot by a fellow cop who had also killed Detective Neal Walker. Not just a cop, but one on her squad. He corrected himself immediately. She knew plenty of other officers in the department. This could be a former patrol partner or supervisor. No one would think twice if he—or she—kept following up on Abby's welfare.

Trouble was, Caleb didn't believe that. Odds were against her partner having known the same officers outside their unit well at all. He might not even have recognized them; KCPD had over thirteen hundred officers last he'd known.

From what Abby had said, Neal had been both dismayed and alarmed by whatever it was he'd stumbled across. Unless Donahue wasn't saying, her partner hadn't confided in his commanding officer.

Although it was possible he had, giving the sergeant a reason to jump to the conclusion that she was the bad apple.

Yeah, but then why hadn't he told his good buddy Caleb the real backstory? Because he didn't want to believe some bad stuff had been going on beneath his nose? Yeah, and if he could lay it at Abby's feet, he could relax. None of the detectives he'd worked with for years could possibly have gone over to the dark side. Had to be the newcomer.

Sad to say, Caleb could even sympathize with that kind of self-deception. Looking at men and women you thought you knew inside and out and realizing one of them was willing to betray his honor and integrity for money?

Yeah, that would be tough.

All the same, somewhere along the line, Caleb had lost his respect for the big, tough Irishman he'd trusted more times than he could count. Donahue had taken the easy out, and in doing so had hurt the woman Caleb loved. Any confusion over who owned his loyalty was long gone.

Unable to resist, he sat on the edge of the bed and gently stroked a lock of blond hair from Abby's face. He felt her stillness, the new tension in her body, just before her eyes opened and fastened onto him. And then she relaxed, smiling. So beautiful in a peaceful moment.

"Caleb," she murmured.

"Sleeping beauty." He planted a hand on the bed and leaned over to kiss her forehead, her cheek, the tip of her nose, and finally her lips. With his body stirring and a groan rumbling in his chest, it was all he could do to pull back, but he made himself. She'd taken a battering today. The last thing she needed was him putting his hands on her.

Although, damn, he did want to.

"Dinner will be ready in about five minutes," he said. "Courtesy of Nancy and my microwave."

Abby's chuckle warmed him deep inside. "And here I expected you to cook for me."

"Oh, I'll do that. But your aunt wouldn't take a *no, thanks* from me."

"Feeding people well is her mission in life." She swept the room with a glance. "Wow. I didn't think I could fall asleep."

"You needed it." He sounded gruff as he pushed himself to his feet. "We'll eat in the kitchen. Come

on down when you're ready." He walked out before
he surrendered to his real hunger.

DINING TOGETHER ALONE with Caleb, rather than surrounded by family, felt surprisingly comfortable even
as Abby was conscious of all the eddies of underlying emotion. The familiar taste of her aunt's fried
chicken and warm potato salad helped. And since
she'd missed lunch, she dug in with enthusiasm, as
did Caleb.

With the table round, they sat close enough to
touch. In fact, his knee brushed hers. He'd produced
beautiful china with gilt edges for this casual meal.
Abby liked it but finally said, with an effort at light-
ness, "I expected mismatched plates."

"Plates?" He looked at his as if he'd never seen
it. "Oh, Mom gave me ten place settings, including
serving dishes." He shrugged, although a small smile
played on his mouth. "At least it's plain. Pink roses,
I might have had to thank her and hide them at the
back of a dark cupboard."

"Would have threatened your masculinity for
sure," she teased sarcastically. "Still, these are pretty
fancy."

"My mother said she has a couple of sets left even
after she gave these to me and another set to my sister. Good God, probably to my brother, too." The
thought seemed to amuse him. "Truth is, my mother
loves flea markets, yard sales, auctions—you name
it. She produced half the furniture in this house. The

dresser in your room—how could she *not* buy it, she said, when the price was so ridiculously low?"

Abby laughed, relaxing. "I've never been much for shopping. I guess between not having a mother to show me the way and spending a lot of time in an Amish household, that's no surprise. Because of my *grossmammi* and then Aenti Nancy, I can cook, but everything is calorie laden."

"I'd get fat in a hurry if I ate three meals a day at your aunt's table," he agreed. "I'm competent in the kitchen thanks to my mother, who insisted my brother and I had to learn to cook and wash dishes just like Susan did, but except for my days off, I depend on my microwave more than Mom would like."

"You've never been married?" That just slipped out, but Abby congratulated herself on how casual it sounded.

"Never even came close." He watched her intently. "You know you have to tell me about your mother eventually, right?"

Of course he'd been wondering. In fact, he'd probably already guessed. Still, she took the last bite of food on her plate, a sweet-onion salad, forced herself to swallow, and set down her fork.

"Mom was shot." She made a face. "Like mother, like daughter, huh? Except Mom…" Her shoulders wanted to hunch, but with an effort she relaxed them. "She was gentle and kind and forgiving. She didn't leave the Amish faith out of disbelief. She loved Dad."

Caleb was holding her hand, she realized, which felt right. His dark green eyes stayed on her face.

"She and Dad were coming home from an evening with some friends, and he stopped at a convenience store for gas. Mom went in to pay."

She could tell he knew what was coming.

"She walked right into the middle of a holdup. I guess she surprised the guy. He shot her, then freaked and shot the clerk, too. He got away with fifty-something dollars."

"I'm so sorry," Caleb said gently.

She forced out a husky, "Yeah, me, too. The guy shot toward Dad, too, but missed. He ran around the side of the store into the alley and disappeared. He'd kept his head ducked so the cops couldn't isolate a good image from the camera over the cash register." Abby had to clear her throat. "Mom died right away, the clerk a day later. Dad haunted the police station for a long time, but no suspect was ever identified. He…never got over it. Even now, I think his body goes through the motions of living, but his mind is not really in there. You know?"

The turbulence in his eyes, Abby recognized. It echoed the bewilderment and hurt and even anger she'd felt then, and to this day, because her father didn't love her enough to stay with her, even to *try* to give her what she'd needed. He'd all but abandoned her, without doing so in a way anyone else but her Amish family would recognize.

Caleb bowed his head for a minute. When he

looked back at her, she understood that he'd needed to gain control so he didn't say things that might hurt her.

"Not hard to figure out why you became a cop," he said roughly. "Did your Amish family understand?"

"With their heads, but not their hearts. They kept reminding me that I need to forgive."

"'Vengeance is mine…saith the Lord.'"

"More that we must forgive, as God forgives us. Vengeance isn't the Amish way—you know that."

"I do." His eyes met hers. "Right this minute, vengeance has some real appeal."

"I've asked myself a thousand times what I'd do if I came face-to-face with the guy who shot my mother, a woman who was no threat to him at all. I'm still not sure," she admitted. "I know I wouldn't kill him if I could help it, but I want to see him spend the rest of his life in a prison cell, with no hope of ever walking out. He was…slight. They could tell that much from the camera footage. He might have been a kid. Aenti Nancy would say, *So troubled, so young.*"

"So vicious, so young."

She nodded. "I wonder how many more people he's killed since then."

"He may be in prison by now, you know. If they didn't get fingerprints from that convenience store…"

"He wore gloves."

"Then any later arresting officers would never have tied him to your mother's murder."

"That's true." Abby huffed, not quite a laugh. "Thinking you're right is all the comfort I'll ever get."

"Damn, Abby." He pushed back his chair to stand and pulled her up into his arms.

Abby wrapped hers around his waist and laid her cheek against his shoulder. Caleb didn't say any more, only held her, one hand moving in soothing circles on her back, his breath stirring loose strands of her hair.

THEY STARTED THE next day at the scene of the crime: the alley where she'd been shot. Caleb would have understood if Abby was a little spooked by returning to the otherwise deserted alley and staring down at a rusty stain in the asphalt that was very likely her partner's blood. Instead, she seemed intensely focused in the way of the homicide detective she'd been.

There was a moment he didn't keep it together as well as he should have. She pointed out where she'd fallen, and he studied the corner of the nearest dumpster. His eye caught on a dark streak where her head had likely hit, and his muscles locked. He stared, unable to look away, for longer than was wise. Only her voice broke the spell.

"I thought being here might nudge my memory, but…" She shrugged.

"Let's go into the bar," he said shortly.

The bartender on shift had heard all the talk at the time but hadn't been working that night. The owner came out of his office in back to study them with suspicion even as he grudgingly offered his name, Brad Spooner.

"I've talked to more cops about that episode than I ever wanted to see in my lifetime. No offense," he added. "Who are you two?"

"I'm Detective Baker," Abby said. "My partner and I were shot back there. He died—I didn't."

Spooner professed not to have any idea what went on behind his business. Yeah, she looked familiar, he admitted grudgingly. He guessed she and her partner might have come in here, but if they'd talked to anyone, it must have been one of the bartenders, not him.

Back in Caleb's vehicle, Abby said, "Once he knew who I was, he got squirrelly."

"I noticed." Caleb pulled out into traffic. "And I'm willing to bet he's on the phone right now telling someone we were there asking questions."

"I'd give a lot to know *who* he called."

"You and me both." Caleb took his eyes off the rearview mirror, satisfied nobody had followed them. "Where next?"

Next turned out to be the backside of an enormous building in the warehouse district near the river. This, she said, was where Neal had taken her when he met with what she'd taken as a crime boss surrounded by thugs.

His reluctance growing by the minute, Caleb contemplated several expensive sedans and SUVs, all black, parked back here. They couldn't have looked more out of place, given the abandoned feel here and the crumbling brick wall of the building punctuated only by a couple of closed steel doors. Not a single window. Their arrival wouldn't have gone unnoticed, however. In one glance, he spotted three cameras.

"I shouldn't do this, but I'm going to give you my backup piece." He lifted the leg of his trousers and removed the small handgun from the holster.

She palmed it quickly and slipped it into her waistband at the small of her back. He'd been glad that morning to see that she wore a linen shirt over a camisole. Despite the heat, he kept on a long-sleeve khaki shirt over a T-shirt for the same reason.

"Ready?"

"You bet." No show of nerves.

He'd seen her soft side. Today, he was getting a better look at the gutsy woman who'd been a decorated cop and made detective at a young age.

He could smell the river but not see it. Heat shimmered around them as they walked across the cracked cement to the nearest door, where he pushed a button that was presumably a doorbell.

A big man with a scar on his neck opened the door within seconds. He took in Abby's more visible bruises and scrapes. "What'ya want?"

"To speak to your boss," she said coolly.

The door closed in their faces.

"He recognized you," Caleb murmured.

"I think he was one of the men there that day," she said as softly.

Not two minutes later, the door swung open again. Mr. Charming snapped, "He'll see you."

A short hall led into a huge open space. Stacked crates lined both sides of the room. The man who waited wore, incongruously, a polo shirt with a discreet label on the chest, chinos with knife-edge creases and athletic shoes. None of that lessened Caleb's impression that this was a man very capable of brutality. The employee who'd shown them in had retreated behind them; three others formed a semicircle with their boss at the center. The small hairs on Caleb's body prickled. They shouldn't have walked into this. His hand wanted to edge for the butt of his gun, but he knew that would be a mistake. A fatal one.

"I've seen you before," the boss said with no particular interest. "You're the woman cop."

"That's right. You spoke to my partner, Neal Walker."

"I heard he was killed."

"He was. That's why I'm here."

"Got nothing to do with us."

"Will you tell me what Neal asked you?"

He blinked a couple of times, the only change of expression he'd so far displayed. "You think it has something to do with the two of you getting shot."

She stayed calm, back straight, looking the man in the eyes. "Yes."

One of the thugs off to the side said, "Twenty minutes."

The boss grunted. "Kid has a soccer game this afternoon."

Well, there was a picture: Daddy in the stands cheering on his daughter. Caleb stayed impassive.

"Guess there's no harm. He thought there was a cop involved with a crime syndicate." His mouth had a small twist, as if he enjoyed putting it that way. "Me, I'm a businessman. There are occasions when I might be willing to pay for a small favor, but what he was talking about—" He shook his head. "I don't know anything about it, and that's the truth."

"You haven't heard rumors?"

"Nah. I told him to look at some of the biker gangs fighting over the city." His gaze flicked from her to Caleb and back. "Now, you'll need to excuse me." Without acknowledging Abby's thanks, he nodded toward the guy behind Caleb.

Without a word, the guy led them back the way they'd come, staying in the open doorway to watch them walk to the SUV. The skin crawled between Caleb's shoulder blades, but by the time he unlocked and got in, the door was closed and they were alone.

The first thing Abby said was, "A youth soccer game."

"If I were that coach, I'd give his kid all the playing time her heart desires."

Abby's laugh was just a little over the top. Caleb grinned at her, relief at making it out of the warehouse, safe, as good as a shot of whiskey.

Chapter Thirteen

Abby strode into the kitchen where Caleb was slicing chicken breasts he intended to stir-fry.

"We're wasting our time," she announced, then swung around and stalked back out. She'd been pacing and venting ever since they got home from their second day exploring the dark side of Kansas City.

Caleb's tension had all gone to his neck today and was refusing to release its grip. The fact that neither of them had any jurisdiction had increasingly nagged at him. On the job was different; as civilians, they'd been at much higher risk going to the places they had, outnumbered by the pimps, bikers, drug dealers and assorted other upstanding citizens of the great state of Missouri they'd sought out for chats.

Cutting meat with a sharp butcher knife was one way to expel some of his frustration and the anxiety balling in his gut. What if they'd ended up in a shoot-out? He'd tried to make her wear the bulletproof vest he carried in the back of his SUV, but she'd refused.

"Anyone we talk to would notice it," Abby had pointed out.

He reminded her that a vest had saved her life not very long ago. When she dug in her heels, he declined to wear the damn thing, either. Maybe she wasn't the only stubborn one in this relationship.

Now, when he heard her returning footsteps, he said, "You're right," and used the knife to slide the chicken strips into a bowl before thoroughly washing both it and the cutting board. "Why would anyone be honest with us?"

"Obviously, they're not being," she retorted sharply.

He reached for a bell pepper. *Whack. Whack.* "We've stirred the pot, which isn't all bad. Whoever is after you knows now that you remember what Neal was doing leading up to the shooting. The scumbag has to be wondering if your memory isn't coming back."

"All the more reason to take me out."

"Which gives me an idea I don't like." A few more *whacks* didn't prevent the muscles in his shoulders and neck from cranking another notch tighter.

She'd stopped pacing, but hadn't sat down, either.

Onion in one hand, Caleb turned to face her.

Her stress showing on her face in a way she hadn't let anyone else see, Abby said, "A trap."

He should have kept his mouth shut, he told himself, but knew she'd have come up with the same plan soon. Truth was, they'd been stumbling around in the dark. He'd gone along with it primarily in hopes either a place or person they encountered would nudge open the floodgates in her mind.

During the drive home from Kansas City this afternoon, he had stolen a few looks at her and wondered if it wasn't doing just that. If those gates weren't quaking even now, her will doing battle with a subconscious part of her brain determined to *keep* them closed.

Last night, the two of them had stopped for dinner on the way home at the café in town. The chances of being overheard had been good, so they'd set aside the subject of what they'd been up to. He'd talked more than she had, telling stories about his boyhood and pranks he and his friends pulled their senior year of high school. Half a dozen people had stopped by the table to say hello, necessitating introductions. He'd watched her closing herself in. In fact, the minute they'd gotten home, she'd said abruptly, "I need a shower, and then I think I'll read in bed."

When he'd followed her upstairs an hour later, he'd seen a light beneath her door. His feet had stopped right outside it. His awareness acute, he'd wondered if she was holding her breath as she waited to see what he'd do.

Caleb had gritted his teeth and reminded himself, over and over again, that she was working her way around to trusting him. Pushing her now would be the mistake of a lifetime.

He hadn't seen her again until this morning.

Today, her face had become increasingly drawn,

as if flesh was melting from her cheeks. She rubbed her temples when she thought he wouldn't notice. During lunch, she slipped a pill in her mouth. Sure as hell, she was feeling those spikes driving into her skull.

Suddenly angry, he said, "You've had a headache for two days. Why are you so determined to hide it?"

Her eyes widened. "How do you know?"

"I'm observant." She fascinated him, which meant his awareness stayed active.

"Oh." As if her knees had given out, she dropped onto a chair in the alcove. "I've…actually felt a little better this afternoon."

"Because you took pain meds."

Studying him warily, she said, "Yes."

"Damn." He set down the onion and went to her, bending to kiss her forehead. "I'm sorry. I shouldn't have gone on the attack."

"No, it's okay." Her smile took an obvious effort. "This was probably a dumb idea from the beginning. I really appreciate you going along with it. We got ourselves into some situations that would have freaked me out if I'd been alone."

He could freak out just thinking of her alone in that warehouse, or at the biker bar that had been part of today's investigative activities.

Fortunately, she didn't seem to notice his reaction and continued talking. "If Neal had learned anything substantive when he was asking questions, I think he'd have told me. He may have caught some hints that worried him, but if so… I didn't yesterday or today."

"They all wanted to steer us in another direction." They should be looking at bikers. A pimp over on Garfield. No, no, back to Independence Avenue. They'd covered a lot of ground today.

"Not hard to see why." She sagged in the chair as if someone had let out the air.

"No." He pulled a chair close to hers so he could hold her hands. She'd acquired a few calluses from her work at the farm, and he moved his thumbs soothingly on her palms while continuing, "I think your partner died because he did the same thing we did, making it plain he was onto something. With him gone, you recovering your memories was the only threat…until now. We've agreed the killer knows what we've been up to. This has to be déjà vu for him."

Alarm widened her eyes. "You're wearing a target now, too."

"Probably not, unless we stumbled too close." And how would they know? They were in the dark as much as they'd been two days ago.

Her hands tightened on his. "Maybe we should call Sergeant Donahue and tell him what we suspect."

"No," Caleb said flatly. "If he hasn't thought of this himself, he's wearing blinders. If he has… I don't like it that he didn't tell me."

"You don't think…"

The suggestion disturbed Caleb on a fundamental level. He shook his head, even as he said, "No, but at this point, we can't rule him out. I don't like that he zeroed in on you so fast."

"It never made sense. If nothing else, Neal wouldn't have taken me along when he talked to people if he'd suspected me at all."

"No." Damn it, he'd known Donahue for a long time, never had even a grain of suspicion that the guy cared enough about money to violate his integrity. A voice inside murmured, *Yeah, but did he ever invite you to his home for a backyard barbecue or to have a few beers and watch a game?* No, he hadn't. In fact, Caleb could only recall meeting Mike's wife a couple of times. Had Donahue kept everyone at a distance?

That was good reason for his current uneasiness. Cops socialized with each other. Their friends were other cops, because their day-to-day experiences separated them from civilians. You couldn't talk about your work with someone who wouldn't understand why you'd drawn on someone that day, or how you'd felt when you arrested an abusive man and then got a good look at a whimpering little girl with pleading eyes and third-degree burns from her daddy dumping boiling water over her as punishment for staying underfoot when he'd told her to get lost.

Caleb's phone rang at that moment, and he wasn't at all surprised to see that the caller was his good friend, Mike Donahue. He was surprised Donahue hadn't called yesterday. He tipped the phone so Abby could see the screen before he answered.

"Mike."

"What the hell have you been up to?" Donahue roared. "You're way out of line poking around in *my* city. Let me tell you—"

Seeing Abby flinch at the bellow, Caleb interrupted without compunction. "I was helping Detective Baker get answers. We're both hoping that revisiting some scenes will help her recover her memory. Isn't that what you want?"

"I want you to leave the damn investigation to us! You're a small-town sheriff now, remember?"

"County." It was a nitpicking thing to quibble over, but Caleb didn't appreciate condescension.

"What?" Suddenly off-stride, Donahue sounded confused.

"County sheriff."

A smile flickered on Abby's lips.

"What the flippin' difference does it make?" Donahue shot back. "Just tell me this. Why didn't you do me the courtesy of letting me know what you planned?"

If Caleb had gone to Kansas City to interview a witness or suspect in a crime that had taken place here in Hearn County, he would have notified KCPD, so Donahue wasn't out of line to ask.

But all Caleb said was a mild "Thought we might stumble across something you haven't."

"You think I'm incompetent? Is that it?"

"What are you complaining about? You wanted me to get close to Abby. I've done that. In my opinion, which I know you don't want to hear, she was a victim at that scene, probably as in the dark about why it happened as you are. But you're hot on her remembering, so we made the decision to push a little, not wait patiently for her memories to return. Which they may never do."

There was a long silence. Donahue had moderated his voice when he said, "I take it your efforts didn't accomplish anything."

Caleb met Abby's eyes. As if she read his mind, she nodded. Time to bait the first hook.

"Not sure. She's getting flashes. Nothing important yet, or I'd have let you know, but I think maybe whatever is blocking her is getting ready to blow."

This pause didn't last quite as long, but Caleb imagined that Donahue was using it for some intensive thinking. So was he.

"Maybe I should try talking to her again," the sergeant said. "She's still with her weird family, right?"

Caleb did not like the casually thrown-out line. Apparently he wasn't the only one fishing. "No, I guess I haven't kept you up to date. A shooter had another go at her. Wounded her aunt, grazed Abby's arm. Not wanting to endanger her family anymore, she took off on her own. I caught up just as two men tried to abduct her. This is serious stuff going on, Mike. Tell me you've been straight with me."

"Of course I have!" Donahue snapped. "What are you implying?"

"That you may think I don't have to know everything."

"You don't."

Having Abby sitting right here listening in, never looking away from him, helped Caleb keep a short rein on his temper. "How did you hear that we'd been in town talking to people?" he asked.

"You two stuck out a little, you know. People tell me things."

"Pimps? Mobsters? Drug dealers?"

"We heard from a couple CIs," he said curtly.

Caleb supposed that it was barely possible he and Abby had spoken to a confidential informant or two.

"I'm making dinner," he said. "Is that all you wanted?"

"I want to know where she is," Donahue said in a hard voice.

"Tonight's temporary. I'll let you know once we find a better place."

"You do that."

Hearing dead air, Caleb dropped his phone on the table. "Guess we're not best friends anymore."

She frowned. "I couldn't hear most of what he said."

"He didn't like us butting in where we don't belong. He wants to keep tabs on you." Caleb shrugged. "I think that's the gist."

"Did you expect different?"

He rubbed the back of his neck. "He should want you to regain your memory."

Still looking perturbed, Abby said, "The thing is, he's already made up his mind about me. Would he believe I'm telling the truth if I did claim to have remembered everything?"

Caleb grimaced. "I don't know." He pushed himself to his feet. "Let me get back to putting dinner together."

She offered to help and was soon slicing bell peppers while he dealt with the onion and garlic. He liked having her here, working alongside him. She teased him a few times about his domestic skill, asked where to find the can of cashew nuts he needed, heated the few remaining sourdough biscuits from Nancy and set the table. Even throwing out ideas for how to set up a situation where she appeared to be alone and vulnerable beat his usual solitary planning.

Having her here was like slotting the last puzzle piece into place, completing the picture. What he had no idea about was whether it felt as right to her as it did to him.

LAST NIGHT, ABBY had been a coward. How else could she explain why she'd fled upstairs at seven in the evening to hide out in her room? Yes, she'd had a headache, but no worse than she had half the time since the shooting.

Being alone with Caleb this way in his home was

different than their talks on her aunt and uncle's front porch. Then she'd been as conscious of his body, his every expression, the glint in his eyes when he looked at her, but she'd known nothing could happen. Now...they were living together. Temporarily, but still.

If he kissed her now, he could take her upstairs to his bed. She would know how his hands and mouth felt on her breasts, the texture of his chest hair, whether the sharp tug in her lower belly meant anything. She could find out what sex was all about beyond the sharp pain, fumbling and disappointment that was all she knew.

Last night, she'd been confused about her feelings, frustrated by their day, scared to trust Caleb. This evening might be her only chance. Abby had no idea what would happen once their trap closed. If she survived, she'd have to testify in a trial, or multiple trials, which would take her back to Kansas City. She'd need to look for a job, and obviously she couldn't work for him.

She sipped her coffee, hoping she wasn't blushing just because she was *thinking* about sex. Women her age weren't supposed to be so naive. She had no intention of telling him how inexperienced she was, but he'd probably figure it out at her first attack of shyness.

The timid part of her wanted to forget the whole idea. The woman who'd become a cop and was a good one disagreed.

Suddenly, she realized Caleb had been silent for an awfully long time, too. She raised her gaze to find him watching her, his eyes dark and the hand that lay on the table clenched in a fist. He didn't move at all, which meant…he was waiting for her?

She swallowed. "Caleb?"

"I want you," he said roughly. "If you plan to say no, I'd appreciate it if you'd do it now."

Abby shocked herself by not hesitating. "I won't be saying no."

He surged to his feet, his chair rocking as he pulled her up. And then, well, she didn't have to say anything at all.

His kiss started tender, then became greedy and possessive. She held on tight, arms locked around his neck, and kissed him back. Who cared if their teeth clanked, or if she made odd little sounds? When he lifted his head for a moment, it felt natural to slide her lips along the cords of his neck, taste his skin in the vulnerable hollow at the base of his throat. Her toes curled when he trailed his mouth across her cheek to nibble on her earlobe at the same time as his big hands closed over her hips and pulled her against him. She reveled in his strength, in all those muscles.

"Upstairs," he said, as if his patience had frayed.

A shiver traveled down her spine and she nodded. Fortunately, she seemed to be past any doubts. As her arms dropped, he grabbed her hand and led her through the living room to the foot of the stairs. There, they stopped to kiss until her mind just about shut down. She wanted to climb his body, she wanted—

He groaned, lifted his head and started up the stairs. Abby concentrated on the first step, the next. His enormous bed. Where she would take off her clothes and bare her naked body to his eyes. Where *he'd* strip and she'd get her first good look at a fully aroused man.

She had to be far gone, because her curiosity and eagerness let her ignore the tiny flutters of panic. *He hasn't noticed yet.*

Caleb didn't stop until they reached that bed. Then he swept back the covers...and stalled, doing nothing but looking down at her. "You're beautiful," he said, in a deep, ragged voice. "You know, I found photos of you online before I met you. There's one of you in your uniform looking official."

She bobbed her head. She knew the one he meant.

"I kept staring at it. Told myself not to be a fool. Then the first time I met you, you were sitting on the grass blinking up at me." He sounded...bemused.

She'd never felt her heart hammering so hard. Some instinct had her lift her hand to his chest, where she felt an echo. "What?" she whispered.

He shook his head. "I was done for." His control seemed to snap. Breathing harshly, he tore her shirt over her head, fumbled with the button at her waist with one hand and the clasp of her bra with the other.

Abby responded by going for his shirt buttons. She *ached*.

Within minutes they'd shed their clothes. She sucked in her breath at the expression on his face, and good thing, too, because the next second he'd claimed her mouth and breathing was the last thing on her mind.

Despite the raw desperation on his face, he laid her gently on his bed, then set about driving her crazy. Abby moaned at the wet heat and suction of his mouth on her breasts, and writhed when his fingers slid between her thighs. Every barrier she had crashed and went down. She gave in to the need to explore his body, too, and if she was clumsy, it hardly seemed to matter. The flex of powerful muscles at her every touch made *her* feel powerful.

He talked, telling her again how beautiful she was, how perfect, groaned when she found sensitive places on his body, murmured, "Yes, like that. Damn." And then, "Are you on birth control?"

"I…" Abby moistened her lips. "No. I didn't think—"

"I have something." He closed his eyes tight. "Just…give me a second."

While she lay still, he pushed himself up and headed into the bathroom. Cupboard doors slammed and he swore creatively. At last he reappeared, packets in his hand. Abby gaped as he walked toward her, confident in his body, although why wouldn't he be? He had that male saunter down, and his erection hadn't subsided.

Abby gulped.

She'd tensed enough that he started over, lavishing attention to her breasts, stroking her until her hips rose and fell and she forgot her worries and just about everything else.

She vaguely heard him tear the packet open. The next thing she knew, he was between her thighs, thrusting into her. Her first thought was that he didn't fit. Her breath caught and she must have stiffened. But he kept pushing until he was seated deep. To her astonishment, it felt good. Really good. She wanted more.

"Please." Abby clutched at his broad back and planted her feet on the mattress to push her hips upward. "Don't stop."

He made a sound she couldn't have described. With his weight on one elbow, he lifted her thigh and kept moving. Almost out, then slow and deep. Abby felt increasingly frantic, needing him to do *something*.

Whatever magical thing it was, he did, because pleasure exploded through her in a way she couldn't have imagined. She heard herself crying out even as Caleb drove hard once more, twice, and she felt throbbing within as he buried his face in the curve of her neck and let himself go.

Abby's hands slipped off the damp expanse of his back, as if she'd lost all ability to move.

THERE WAS ONLY a buzz in his head. He'd never felt anything like this before. Moving ever again didn't seem likely.

The idea that he might be crushing her was his first coherent thought. Yeah. Had to roll over. It felt like a huge effort when he did.

As his mind cleared, he remembered how exquisitely tight she was.

He pushed up so he could see her face. "You weren't a virgin."

She gazed back with defiance. "Was I supposed to be?"

"I wondered. That's all."

"Because I blush?"

He smiled at her. "Partly that."

"I'm not very experienced." Her lips pinched. "I guess you could tell."

"No."

"Oh." She eyed him. "I had a boyfriend in college. Everyone else was having sex, and I wanted to fit in. To be modern. So..." Her shoulders moved. "It was only a few times, and not that great."

"That's it? A few times?"

"I never really wanted to try again." Her cheeks glowed red.

"So what was this? An experiment?"

Abby gaped at him, then exclaimed, "No!" She shoved him and tried to roll free. He recaptured her effortlessly.

"What, then?"

"It was you! That's what. But you don't have to take this as some...some hearts and flowers thing. It's not. Until now, I didn't want to try this again, okay?"

"This?" That ticked him off. "Make love, you mean."

After a moment, her face softened. "Yes."

"Don't discount me or yourself." He relented enough to kiss her before forcing himself to release her and roll off the bed. He needed to ditch the condom so they could start all over again.

Knowing she couldn't see, Caleb smiled wryly at himself. He liked knowing she'd only had one lover before, and that one not very satisfactory. He'd never felt quite so primitive before. Abby had brought him all kinds of new experiences.

Chapter Fourteen

Abby shaped a sheet of dough over an enormous heap of peeled and sliced apples in a pie pan. From long practice, she deftly united the bottom and top pie crusts, cut a tic-tac-toe design in the top that would vent the heat, and used a fork to flute the edges. Repeat, and she had two pies ready to go in the oven.

Once that was done and she'd set a timer, she began to clean up. Somehow, she'd been consigned to KP duty for herself and her around-the-clock bodyguard, Deputy John Wisniewski. Didn't it figure. His excuse was that he'd never cooked without electrical appliances. The real reason, she quickly figured out, was that his wife waited on him hand and foot.

Since she'd baked bread this morning and chili simmered on the stove, she was done until they'd both eaten. Which they wouldn't do together; one of them needed to be on guard all the time.

Even now, with John prowling this floor of the house, Abby kept Caleb's small backup handgun, a

Ruger 9mm, on the table within easy reach. Fortunately, they'd had a chance to drive to a range for her to try the gun out, so it didn't feel completely unfamiliar when she picked it up.

While the pies baked, she supposed she'd go upstairs and peek from the crack between curtains toward the woods behind her cousin Rose's house. No, she'd scan every direction, watch for movement, for anything that didn't belong.

What else was there to do? She couldn't concentrate enough to read, not when her ears were tuned for the tiniest of sounds, not when even John's soft footfall would make her head snap up.

Abby had forgotten the sheer boredom that was a major part of most stakeouts. Somehow, you were supposed to stay alert for mind-numbing hours on end.

The place for her to hole up had been her suggestion. Her cousin Rose was having a hard time carrying twins as her due date drew nearer. Her doctor had ordered restricted activity. Nobody would be surprised that Rose and Matthew had gone to stay with her parents, Rose's pregnancy their excuse. "She is best off with her *mamm* and *daad*," Nancy had insisted to anyone who asked. Abby had expected to resume her Amish garb, but Caleb didn't want her to step a foot outside and had ordered her to keep curtains pulled. In other words, it didn't matter what she wore, since no one but he and the deputy were supposed to see her. She could move more freely without skirts.

"We want them to commit by breaking in," he told her. She had hidden a shudder. Glass shattering as someone came in a window, or the sound of wood splintering when a door was kicked open. An Amish farmhouse wasn't exactly a fortress.

This wouldn't have worked if Matthew had farmed, but the property was small and he worked at a cabinet-making shop in Ruston. At Caleb's suggestion, the milk cow and small flock of chickens had gone with Rose and Matthew. That way no one had to take care of them. Caleb refused to put anyone else in a position to be used as bait to draw Abby outside.

It had taken twenty-four hours after he and Abby laid the plans for them to gain permission first from Abby's family, then from the bishop of their church district. Given that the Amish wanted nothing to do with violence, subterfuge or police operations, Abby was surprised when Samuel Troyer agreed. It helped that he had known her since she was a girl and been kept informed of the attempts on her life. That those men who were determined to kill her had been willing to shoot Nancy had shocked him deeply.

Within twenty-four hours, Caleb had left her here with the deputy he said was his most capable. John was in his midthirties, Abby guessed, a stocky man of about her own height, seeming dour at first meeting. Given that the two of them had been alone in the house for going on three days now, they'd gotten to know each other. He told her he'd started his career with the St. Joseph PD but married his high school sweetheart and decided to come home to Ruston when a job became available so they'd be near both their families.

She really didn't want him to be hurt or killed because of her. How would she tell his wife, now pregnant with their second child?

She and John kept watch during the daytime. Mostly John, because *somebody* had to prepare meals and his professed ineptness made that her. Once darkness fell, Caleb would steal across the fields and quietly let himself in the front door. At near-dawn, he'd wake them before he slipped out. If he was getting any sleep at all, Abby couldn't figure out how. She wasn't doing all that well herself.

Adrenaline had pumped through her the first day. Hard to forget that *she* was the goat staked out to draw a predator, which made this a tiny bit different than the usual dull police stakeouts she'd done. It also made it next to impossible to snuggle into bed and get a good night's sleep, even if Caleb was downstairs standing guard.

By the second day, anxiety and eagerness mutated into impatience.

By this morning, she'd been flat-out bored.

Maybe this trap wasn't going to work. For all they knew, armed men were still watching her aunt and uncle's farm instead. Caleb had felt sure that any interested party would note that Rose and Matthew had oh-so-conveniently vacated this house. He'd made sure there was talk of it in town at the café, the grocery store, anywhere outsiders might overhear. And of course, he'd let Donahue know where she was, offering him the chance to interview her again.

So far he hadn't accepted the offer, apparently relying on Caleb's reports. They were counting on him having told Sam Kirk, at the least, where she could be found, if not other detectives in the squad.

John interrupted her brooding by entering the kitchen at that moment. "Smells good," he said quietly.

"The chili is ready anytime. I'm going upstairs, if that's okay."

His eyes narrowed on her face. Did he think she was going nuts? If so, he might be right. But all he did was nod. "Must be hot as Hades up there."

It was, she discovered. Today had been uncomfortably hot, the air feeling heavy, the weight almost literal. Trudging up the steps required an effort. Abby was reminded of the day Aenti Nancy had been shot. Whether from nature or man, she had a feeling of impending danger.

The gun in one hand, she shifted the curtain an inch or two so she could peek out the window in the bedroom she was using. Feeling stifled, she'd have given a lot to shove it open. Of course she couldn't do that; the house was supposed to appear unoccupied or as if somebody was trying very hard to make it *appear* vacant. Besides, even the leaves on the trees she could see hung limply. There couldn't be any breeze at all.

The woods and fields were bone-dry; a lightning storm could ignite fires. The sky had a yellowish tinge that made her think about tornadoes, too. Did this house have a storm cellar? She should have asked. Hey, it could have served as a panic room, too.

With a sigh, she let the curtain fall, made her rounds and went back downstairs.

The pies still had twenty minutes to go. John sat down with a bowl of chili while she prowled the downstairs in his place, straining to hear any sounds from outside, even more cautiously stealing looks.

Despite her lack of appetite, she made herself eat a little when her turn came. She wished darkness would fall so Caleb would come. Even though they wouldn't be able to do much more than talk quietly for a few minutes, something in her settled when he was here. He hadn't kissed her when John might see them, so mostly she felt lucky when he brushed his hand over hers, or their eyes met and she saw that his frustration and worry was as great as hers, that he wanted to put his arms around her.

How long could they keep this up? What if no attack happened? Maybe Caleb had a plan B, but if so he hadn't mentioned it, and she surely didn't.

When the timer went off and she removed the pies from the oven, she glanced at the clock. Sunset came at about six forty-five right now, so Caleb should get here in about an hour.

Patience, she counseled herself.

EYE ON THE CLOCK, Caleb gobbled the beef Stroganoff he'd heated in the microwave. Abby seemed to be filling her time doing some baking with ingredients she found in her cousin's pantry or that he brought for her, so he could pretty well count on dessert there. He'd have eaten whatever she put in front of him no matter what, because it seemed to please her to see him enjoying the product of her labor. He guessed some of her aunt's determination to feed everyone had rubbed off on Abby. That, or she was combating the feeling of helplessness that would be natural in her situation.

He felt helpless, too. He didn't like trusting her safety to anyone else, however reliable and experienced. Caleb had seriously considered taking vacation and letting everyone assume he'd gone out of town while he was holed up with Abby, but he had so damn much on his plate these days, he couldn't. He didn't believe the assault would come during the day, anyway. Taking potshots at her from the woods was one thing, but if he were planning a break-in, he'd wait for darkness.

Which was nearly here, he saw with a glance through the window. He cleaned up quickly and put on his vest over his uniform shirt. He'd ordered both

Abby and John to wear theirs even when sleeping, however tempting it would be in this hot, humid weather to take them off.

Caleb had just gotten into his SUV when his cell phone rang. Crap—the number belonged to dispatch. "Tanner," he said.

"Sheriff, there was a hit-and-run out on Methany Road."

Caleb braced himself, hearing the stress in the evening dispatcher's voice.

"Three boys riding their bikes. A car sideswiped them all."

"Dead or injured?"

She didn't yet know. Given the address, he paused only long enough to text John Wisniewski. Traffic accident, will be late.

Then he accelerated onto the road, praying none of those boys had died.

By the time he arrived, dusk was cutting down on visibility. He couldn't miss the blinking lights from emergency vehicles, though. Caleb parked behind a sheriff's-department unit, jumped out and strode forward to join the cluster of uniformed personnel looking at the twisted frame of a bike on the right shoulder.

"Sheriff," one of his deputies said in relief. Carson Myrick, only twenty-four years old, but on the job three years now.

"What happened?"

 ͡n as he bent his head to listen, he saw one

boy sitting at the edge of the ditch, curled forward in pain or distress. A female EMT crouched next to him, her hand on the boy's arm.

"Jeffrey Groendyke—" the deputy nodded that way "—was in the lead. He had time to throw himself off his bike into the ditch. He swears the driver never braked. He says he and his two friends were riding single file—there was plenty of room to pass them. For some reason, the car drifted."

Caleb knew a Walter Groendyke, a dentist. This had to be his kid. "Teenagers?"

"He doesn't think so. It was a dark-colored sedan, he thinks black, and he saw the driver's head from the back, but no one else."

Caleb drew a deep breath. "The other two boys?"

"Already being transported." Myrick was holding himself together, but now the muscles in his jaw spasmed. "Broken bones, at the least. One of the two, ah, didn't look so good."

"All right," Caleb said. "Let me talk to Jeffrey."

This wouldn't be a quick detour. His gut knotted at the delay, but these kids came first.

ABBY HELD HER BREATH. Holding herself rigidly, she sat in the darkness partway up the staircase, waiting.

Thunder rumbled in the distance. The storm was still too far away for her to have seen the lightning. She let herself breathe again. That's all she'd heard. Thunderstorms came on the heels of oppressively hot days, like this one.

John was downstairs. He'd been displaying some of the same symptoms of growing tension she had. Caleb's text had ratcheted up her uneasiness, and maybe John's, too.

Reason said they were both experienced cops, and armed. On the thought, she wrapped her fingers around the butt of the Ruger that lay on her lap. She hoped and prayed she'd never have to fire it, or the rifle in her bedroom, but tonight, keeping it close was a comfort.

John had positioned her here, where she could retreat upstairs if she heard shots.

"It's you they're after," he'd pointed out. "Once someone is in the house, you need to be ready to fight, too, but the head of the stairs is easier to defend."

Sure, but how would she feel if she had to retreat, knowing he was down, wounded or dead? From here, all she could see was the front door and a slice of the living room. After another roll of thunder, she listened for John's footstep—and for any other sounds.

Gunfire, it had occurred to her, could pass unnoticed in the midst of a thunder storm.

A soft scuff came from below. She strained to make out the figure of a man against the darkness.

"Abby?" he whispered.

"Yes?"

"No more word from Caleb."

The past half hour had crept by. He wasn't all that

late. "We're okay," she murmured as much to herself as him, sounding steadier than she felt.

"Sure we are," John agreed, before he merged back into the dark.

CALEB HAD BEEN joined by the deputy he'd promoted to patrol sergeant. A year ago, Raines had completed training from the Missouri State Highway Patrol in accident reconstruction. Caleb had had the initial training himself while he was with KCPD, then taken a more advanced course after he signed on as sheriff. Now, the two of them walked slowly down the two-lane country road, both carrying powerful flashlights that they swept to each side in search of any marks laid down by tires during braking or sharp swerves or turns.

"Damn it," Caleb growled. "The kid's right. He never even applied the brakes."

"Doesn't look like," Sergeant Raines agreed. "How could he not see three boys on bikes? The accident happened during full daylight." Raines lifted his flashlight so the beam spotlighted the torn soil on the road verge and the damaged remnants of two of the three bicycles. "You'd swear this creep hit them on purpose."

Caleb stopped where he was. Ice slid through his blood veins.

This creep hit them on purpose.

What if that's exactly what the driver had done? And what if his goal had nothing to do with the boys?

What if he had wanted to make sure Caleb was too occupied to reinforce the two people who were otherwise alone waiting for the killer and his backup to make their move?

Black sedan—just like the one that had smashed into the buggy and come so close to killing Abby and Joshua.

He yanked out his phone. No missed calls or texts. Good news or bad? He didn't know. He called John… and heard only rings and then voice mail.

"I have to go," he said. "You're in charge." Then he ran, not giving a damn that everyone remaining at the accident site had turned to stare.

A SHOCKING BURST of white light that momentarily blinded Abby and gave her a jolt was followed no more than two or three seconds later by a deep roll of thunder. The storm had come their way and was almost overhead. She hadn't heard any rain slamming onto the roof. They *needed* that rain.

On the heels of the thunder, a hard slam came from the back of the house. She rose to her feet, straining to hear more. That could have been a tree coming down, but she didn't think so.

The crack of a fired handgun came next. A shout. Another shot. More. How many men had come into the house once they kicked the door open? John had to be firing back. *Please let him be all right.*

Her own gun in firing position, Abby backed slowly up the stairs, feeling with each foot for the

Will frowned. "Poppy?" An image appeared of a girl with freckles, braces, skinned knees and reddish-brown hair in pigtails. "I haven't thought of Poppy in years. I thought she moved away."

"She did, but she came back about six months ago and started a catering business in Whitefish," Garrett said. "I only know because I ran into her at a party recently. The food was really good, if that helps."

"Wait, I remember her. Cute kid. Didn't her father work for the forest service?" their younger brother Shade asked as he also came into the kitchen with a box of supplies. He deposited the box inside the large pantry just off the kitchen. "Last box," he announced, dusting off his hands.

"You remember, Will. Poppy and her dad lived in the old forest service cabin a mile or so from here," Garrett said, grinning at him. "She used to ride her bike over here and help us with our chores. At least, that was her excuse."

Will avoided his brother's gaze. It wasn't like he'd ever forgotten.

"I just remember the day she decided to ride Lightning," Shade said. "She climbed up on the corral, and as the horse ran by, she jumped on it!" He shook his head, clearly filled with admiration. "I can't imagine what she thought she was going to do, riding him bareback." He laughed. "She stayed on a lot longer than I thought she would. But it's a wonder she didn't kill herself. The girl had grit. But I always wondered what possessed her to do that."

Garrett laughed and shot another look at Will. "She was trying to impress our brother."

"That poor little girl was smitten," Dorothea agreed as she narrowed her dark gaze at Will. "And you, being fifteen and full of yourself, often didn't give her the time of day. So what could possibly go wrong hiring her to cook for you?"

Don't miss
Stroke of Luck *by B.J. Daniels, available March 2019*
wherever HQN Books and ebooks are sold.

www.Harlequin.com

"Bad luck always comes in threes."

Standing in the large kitchen of the Sterling Montana Guest Ranch, Will Sterling shot the woman an impatient look. "I don't have time for this right now, Dorothea."

"Just sayin'," Dorothea Brand muttered under her breath. The fifty-year-old housekeeper was short and stout with a helmet of dark hair and piercing dark eyes. She'd been a fixture on the ranch since Will and his brothers were kids, which made her invaluable, but also as bossy as an old mother hen.

After the Sterling boys had lost their mother, Dorothea had stepped in. Their father, Wyatt, had continued to run the guest ranch alone and then with the help of his sons until his death last year. For the first time, Will would finally be running the guest ranch without his father calling all the shots. He'd been looking forward to the challenge and to carrying on the family business.

But now his cook was laid up with a broken leg? He definitely didn't like the way the season was starting, Will thought as the housekeeper leaned against the counter, giving him one of her you're-going-to-regret-this looks as he considered who he could call.

As his brother Garrett brought in a box of supplies from town, Will asked, "Do you know anyone who can cook?"

"What about Poppy Carmichael?" Garrett suggested as he pulled a bottle of water from the refrigerator, opened it and took a long drink. "She's a caterer now."

Need an adrenaline rush from nail-biting tales
(and irresistible males)?

Check out **Harlequin Intrigue®**,
Harlequin® Romantic Suspense and
Love Inspired® Suspense books!

New books available every month!

CONNECT WITH US AT:

Facebook.com/groups/HarlequinConnection

 Facebook.com/HarlequinBooks

 Twitter.com/HarlequinBooks

 Instagram.com/HarlequinBooks

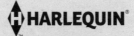 Pinterest.com/HarlequinBooks

ReaderService.com

◈ HARLEQUIN®

**ROMANCE WHEN
YOU NEED IT**

SGENRE2018R

small, in an honorable profession, making a difference in the world.

Now he was faced with the daunting task of job hunting with a huge strike on his record.

But not today.

Why he'd decided to take the train from Bethesda, Maryland, to the political hub of the entire country was beyond his own comprehension. But with nowhere else to go and nothing holding him back—no job, no family, no home—he'd thought, "Why not?"

He'd never been to the White House, never stopped to admire the Declaration of Independence, drafted by the forefathers of his country and he'd never stood at the foot of the Lincoln Memorial, in the shadow of the likeness of Abraham Lincoln, a leader who'd set the United States on a revolutionary course. He'd never been to the Vietnam War Memorial or any other memorial in DC.

Yeah. And so what?

Sightseeing wouldn't pay the bills. Out of the military, out of money and sporting a dishonorable discharge, Declan would be hard-pressed to find a decent job. Who would hire a man whose only skills were superb marksmanship that allowed him to kill a man from four hundred yards away, expertise in hand-to-hand combat and the ability to navigate himself out of a paper bag with nothing more than the stars and his wits?

Don't miss
Marine Force Recon *by Elle James,*
available April 2019 wherever
Harlequin® *Intrigue books and ebooks are sold.*

www.Harlequin.com

Declan O'Neill hiked his rucksack higher on his shoulders
and trudged down the sidewalk in downtown Washington,
DC. The last time he'd seen so many people in one place,
he'd been a fresh recruit at US Marine Corps basic training
in San Diego, California, standing among a bunch of
teenagers, just like him, being processed into the military.

He shouldered his way through the throngs of
sightseers, businessmen and career women hurrying to the
next building along the road. The sun shone on a bright
spring day. Cherry blossoms exploded in fluffy pinkish-
white, dripping petals onto the lawns and sidewalks in an
optimistic display of hope.

Hope.

Declan snorted. Here he was, eleven years after joining
the US Marine Corps…eleven years of knowing what was
expected of him, of not having to decide what to wear each
day. Eleven years of a steady paycheck, no matter how

Get 4 FREE REWARDS!

We'll send you 2 FREE Books
plus 2 FREE Mystery Gifts.

Harlequin Intrigue® books feature heroes and heroines that confront and survive danger while finding themselves irresistibly drawn to one another.

FREE
Value Over
$20

next tread. John had had 9-1-1 dialed on his phone, ready for one push of his thumb to send. Did he have time?

A man's voice called out. Another, pitched lower, answered. She went still, listening.

Quiet after that. Which meant John must be down…unless Caleb had arrived and joined him. She shook her head. They'd have called out to her if that was so. No, she had to assume there were intruders in the house, and she was on her own.

She'd have given almost anything to be able to *see*. Another bolt of lightning would be good—except someone looking up the stairs would see *her*.

Run to get the rifle? But that would mean taking her eyes off the staircase. She should have kept it right here.

She felt strange, almost as if she was looking down at herself. She blinked, saw Neal in the diffuse light from a distant streetlamp and the dim bulb over the back door into the bar. Footsteps. A man walking toward them—

This wasn't the time for a flashback! Abby shook her head hard. Thank God, she'd reached the upstairs hall. All she could hear now was the thud of her heartbeat. She flattened her back against the wall and watched for movement yet saw the alley instead of the green countryside beyond the window. The man strolled casually, not afraid. Better to be cautious. She reached for the butt of her gun, wrapped her fingers around it.

"Where the hell is the light switch?" someone
said downstairs.

That voice.

She was in the alley again. It was as if someone
was flicking back and forth between television channels, sucking her along for the ride.

We've got to quit meeting like this.

Donahue. Why hadn't Neal talked to him at the
station? Why *here*? Or had Neal expected to meet
someone else?

The sergeant walked toward her, shaking his head.
You shouldn't be mixed up in this.

"In what?" She heard her own confusion.

Your partner knows. Sorry, kid. He grabbed her
by the upper arms and slammed her backward. Ex-
cruciating pain. She was falling.

Flick.

No, she stood in the hall, just out of sight of anyone at the foot of the stairs.

"Abby?" Donahue again, but here and now. "I'm
just here to talk, and somebody started shooting at
us."

*Gee, maybe because you kicked your way in in-
stead of knocking?*

"I haven't had time to get up here during the day.
Now that I'm here, can we talk?"

She spoke loudly. "Where's John?"

"Who's that? Oh, the guy who tried to kill me?
He's down, but okay."

"It was you," she said. "You slammed me into the

dumpster then drew my gun and shot Ne~
think I'd never remember?"

"Too bad you lived." He sounded genuinel
gretful. "It would have been quick and easy."

"You were too stupid to notice I wore a vest."

A faint creak served as warning. She'd learned
the sounds of this old house.

"Two more steps, and I'll be able to take your head
off," she snapped. "Don't think I won't."

His gun barked, over and over. Chips of plaster
from the walls and ceiling flew at her.

For the first time outside a range, she pulled the
trigger, heard obscenities. In the ensuing silence,
she heard no thuds to suggest he'd beaten a retreat.
Like her, he'd probably flattened his back against the
wall…or had squatted low, thinking he could creep
high enough to leap up and pepper her with bullets.

Abby took a deep breath and waited, the hands
gripping the Ruger completely steady.

CALEB PARKED ONE property away. Just as he ducked
between boards of a fence, a bolt of lightning lit
the sky and left him momentarily blind. He started
running anyway, accompanied by thunder. A sheet
of rain came out of nowhere, making it harder to
see. He didn't hear anything after the thunder and
couldn't even see the damn house until he was thirty
yards or so away. That's when he saw light moving
in the front room. Flashlight, he knew immediately.
John or Abby might have had reason to use one,

know it would be visible even

had him in its grip, but he still
ough to call dispatch and ask for

lights," he ordered.

Deputy Vogl should be nearest to you."

Damn, the kid.

"Send all available units. Tell deputies to expect to find themselves under fire." Although it would probably all be over before any backup arrived.

Either that or he'd feel foolish when he found John and Abby had turned on a flashlight for a minute to find something one of them had dropped.

He jammed the phone in his pocket, pulled his Glock and broke into a jog. A minute later, he was able to crouch by the porch and hear voices. Two, at least, the rumble too low for him to make out words, but male, both of them.

Caleb made his way around the side of the house, bending over as he passed windows. He was almost to the back door before he saw it swinging open, the wood splintered around the lock.

No mistake, then. The assailants were in the house. Number unknown. *If I'd been here—*

He shook the thought out of his head as he edged up to the door, gently eased it open. No time for that. Despite the lightning, his eyes had adjusted to darkness well enough for him to make out the table and chairs. A shape lay on the floor. A man, but he

couldn't let himself stop. If it was John, there was nothing he could do.

One cautious step after another took him into the short hallway. Right now, he was the next thing to invisible. They wouldn't expect him.

Ahead was the foyer at the foot of the stairs, a dining room to the left, living room to the right. Another few feet and his head would show between banisters on the staircase. Instead, he crouched low, gun in firing position, and listened hard.

ONE OF THE men's voices drifted up to Abby. "What are we waiting for? Three of us, we can overwhelm her. If I use the shotgun, I can blast through walls."

"We need to get this done so we can be out of here." Another voice she didn't know.

"Shotgun makes too much noise. Detective Baker doesn't want to shoot anyone." This was Donahue responding. Thinking she'd surrender? Or was he just taunting her?

A part of her had been angry enough to kill someone for a very long time. *For you, Mom. For John.* Abby took a chance, stepped forward and fired down the staircase. Once, twice, three times. The gun jumped in her hands. There was a crash and yelling down below.

She heard a siren, please, please, coming here. Now there was more swearing.

"We've got to get out of here."

"That bitch got me! I'm bleeding!"

"We can't leave her alive."

"She's your problem," one of the men said. "You take care of her."

Rats fleeing the ship.

A hard *thud*. One of them had gone down. Had she killed one of them? Later she might feel bad, but not yet.

Multicolored flashing lights bounced off the walls Abby could see. A bellow came through a bullhorn.

"Come out with your hands up!"

She pinged another bullet deliberately high.

And then she heard Caleb. "Drop the guns! Now! Hands against the wall."

A gun barked, answered by another.

"Last chance!" he yelled. Then, "Abby? Are you all right?"

"Yes. I'm okay." She let her arms sag so that the Ruger pointed at the floor. She took a deep breath and raised her voice. "I'm fine."

Epilogue

Hours later, Caleb was still having trouble believing that Abby was uninjured, that he'd gotten back in time. Yeah, and that his youngest deputy had done exactly the right thing, at the right moment.

One of the men was in a cell in the small jail in town. Another was in surgery at the hospital to remove a bullet from his shoulder. Donahue was dead. He'd opened fire at Caleb, who had shot him. It might give him some nightmares, but he didn't think so. Mostly, he was glad he'd reacted fast enough and that Abby hadn't had to do something that would haunt her.

John had a whopping bruise on his chest and likely cracked ribs, but had been wearing his vest as ordered. When he fell, he'd hit his head and knocked himself out. Lucky thing, too. If he'd so much as twitched, they'd have kept shooting, and he would be dead. Instead, he'd been admitted at the hospital to be under observation because of a concussion.

Abby and Caleb had finally made it home. His

house. The minute they walked in the door and he turned the deadbolt, he hauled her into his arms. He opened his mouth to tell her she'd scared him, but kissed her instead. Probably savagely, but before he could even try to ease back, she'd risen on tiptoe, thrown her arms around his neck and kissed him with need as desperate. Words weren't what either of them craved, not yet.

He got her out of what looked like ballet shoes and thin knit pants and skimpy panties. Somewhere along the way, she'd removed her Kevlar vest, but he still wore his. In the end, he unbuckled his belt, unzipped his pants and took her up against the door. The tempest inside the house didn't last long. In the end, he fell to his knees, taking her with him. Both lay on their backs, gasping for air.

When he was able to talk, he rolled his head toward her and said, "Hell of a day."

For a moment, she didn't react. Then she snorted— no, laughed. And tears poured down her cheeks even as she kept laughing.

Caleb wrapped his arms around her, pressed his lips to her head and murmured what he hoped were comforting things.

It was a long time before Abby pulled herself together enough to remember she was naked from the waist down and lying on his hardwood floor. Clutching her pants, she fled upstairs, forgetting he could see her backside. Smiling, Caleb got mostly dressed again and went to the kitchen to put on the coffee.

He was so damn tired, he didn't expect it to keep him awake.

By the time it was ready and he had poured two cups, Abby reappeared. He'd heard the shower running but saw that she'd bundled her hair up so it wasn't wet except for some damp tendrils around her face. He leaned back against the counter edge and drank in the sight of her, blush and all.

"It's over," she said. "I can't believe it."

For both of them. He'd called in the Missouri State Highway Patrol Criminal Investigations people, since the crimes spanned counties and he'd shot and killed a fellow law-enforcement officer. They'd learned enough from the first brief interviews with the two men who'd survived to know that Donahue, a man Caleb had respected and even called *friend*, had been involved for years in sheltering a protection racket and prostitution ring operated by a biker gang. Caleb might not regret shooting Donahue, but he'd spend plenty of time wondering how he could have been so blind.

But right now, his life was on the line in a different way. Throat tight, he held out a hand.

Abby came to him still blushing, her gaze shyly lowered, which would have amused him if he hadn't been bone-deep scared. The wild woman who'd held off three gunmen and made frantic love with him against his front door was only one facet of this complex woman.

Closing his hand around hers, he cleared his throat. "I poured you a cup of coffee."

"I saw." She didn't look away from him.

He didn't want to look away from her vivid blue eyes.

Just lay it out there. "I love you," he said hoarsely.

For too many seconds, she just stared. Then she began to cry again, even as she smiled. She used the hem of her shirt to swipe her tears. "Oh, I'm falling apart! I'm so sorry, I've just been so afraid—" She swallowed. "Falling in love with you scared me so much when I didn't know whether I could trust you. Or...or whether you felt even *close* to the same."

"God." He bent his head. "You'll stay with me?"

"Yes, although Aenti Nancy and Onkel Eli won't approve."

When he raised his head again, he saw that a smile trembled on her mouth. She was teasing—although she was right. Her Amish family wouldn't like Abby cohabiting with him. Neither would the conservative voters he'd need to keep himself in office, come to think of it. But he already knew where the two of them were going.

"You know I want to marry you." He tugged until she leaned on him, thighs to breasts. "I'll give you time, but you need to know."

Expression grave, she searched his face. "You've come running every single time I've needed you. I've seen you mad, and laughing and kind. No." For just an instant, the shyness returned. "Tender. I've

seen how your men respect you. Your house tells me about you, too, you know."

"And?"

"I'm twenty-nine, and you're the only man ever I've loved like this. Of course I want to spend the rest of my life with you. How could you think I wouldn't want to marry you?"

Suddenly shaky on his feet, Caleb wasn't sure who was leaning on whom.

"I'll support you whatever you need to do about your career."

Her eyes suddenly had a sheen.

"The rest of our lives," he murmured.

Her arms came around him. "Tonight, I was afraid we wouldn't have that."

"Me, too," he said. "Me, too."

Suddenly, exhilaration burst through him. Who needed coffee? He bent, swept her up in his arms, and carried her upstairs to bed.

* * * * *